# GREEN MANGO MAGIC

# GREEN MANGO MAGIC

## SYLVIE HOSSACK

AN AVON CAMELOT BOOK

AVON BOOKS, INC.
1350 Avenue of the Americas
New York, New York 10019

First Avon Camelot Paperback Printing: October 1999
First Avon Camelot Hardcover Printing: November 1998

CAMELOT TRADEMARK REG. U.S. PAT. OFF. AND IN OTHER COUNTRIES, MARCA REGISTRADA, HECHO EN U.S.A.

Printed in the U.S.A.

OPM 10 9 8 7 6 5 4 3 2 1

For Ian

# Acknowledgments

Thank you to my writing family—my fellow writers in critique, my agent, my editor, and everyone at Avon Books.

To those who inspired this story—my husband who first took me to the islands of his birth; his parents, Grace and Sandy, who welcomed me to their home at Paauhau Sugar Plantation; and our former neighbors on Kolea Road—mahalo.

To Mel Holokahiki Sallas for his favorite green mango recipe; to his wife, Audrey Kapuamaeole M. for those "just right words" in pidgin; to Gini Chapson, Emily Ann Collins, and John A. Hersman, MD, who kindly read an early version of the manuscript; to Jerra Fjelstad, RN, and Nancy D. McLemore for their information about catheter ports; to Ron Bachman for his knowledge about the hunting of feral pigs; to Galen H. Kamishita for sharing his secrets about making maile lei at Kokee; to my husband's classmates, Winston Ing and Eddie Oshiro, for their poetic descriptions of poi; to the Kenneth Chang family and especially Nannette Pualani Dettloff for their aloha—thank you.

# Contents

x

# GREEN MANGO MAGIC

# 1

## Maile

From high on the ridge, Maile could see miles and miles of green sugarcane fields stretching out to the ocean. "Come look, Tutu," she called to her grandmother. She pointed to the sugar plantation town below. "There's Charlie's house and the sugar mill. And in the hills the plantation manager's house." As she leaned into the wind, her Hawaiian dress, her muumuu, flapped against her legs. Long strands of her hair swirled behind her.

"I can even see the coast road. And the Ohana Hotel!"

Tutu Lady stood near the forest, away from the cliffs. "My-lee," she called, "I don't like you so close to the edge."

Hearing her name, Maile turned. "I'll be careful." She took a tiny step farther and looked straight down. There was a whistle of wind below. But in the late morning shadows, the Hawaiian valley where she lived lay hidden by steep lava rock cliffs and the tops of trees. She backed away, a few steps at a time.

Maile jumped off her lava rock lookout, away from the wind. "Wait for me!" She ran to catch up. "I'm coming." Through the trees she spotted her tutu, whose red dress flashed against the green of the forest.

Tutu Lady waited by a small grove of guava trees. On her feet were her rubber thong sandals. Just like Maile's. Her hair was pulled back in a bun, still tidy and neat, with no loose strands. She smiled when Maile joined her. Then they walked together, searching for the green creeper vines they gathered each summer: the maile vine, Maile's namesake. Gathering the vine was Maile's idea, her own tradition. For her mama.

Deep in the forest, they found what they were looking for. Maile peeled the vine off tree branches and the trunks of trees. She and Tutu Lady sat together, the air cool around them. They stripped off the skin of soft green bark from the vine's woody core. They tied short pieces to long pieces. Then Maile twirled ten long strands, the green bark with the leaves still attached, around and around together. Pieces of vine curled around themselves, forming a garland. At least five feet long! And as they worked, Tutu Lady talked story about Maile's mama. Mostly funny stories that made Maile smile. Sometimes, though, a sad feeling seemed to bubble up from nowhere and then she'd turn away so Tutu Lady wouldn't see. And Tutu Lady, her eyes glittering in the light, as if she had tears in them, sometimes turned away, too.

The shiny green maile leaves filled the air with a hint of licorice. That afternoon, the same soft scent drifted into the lobby of the Ohana Hotel as Maile walked through—like a barefoot princess, her hair soft and flowing. She wore a maile lei draped over her shoulders, the two ends of the lei left open, hanging below her knees. Small leis of fern hung around her wrists like bracelets. Her long Hawaiian dress swirled around her ankles.

She paused near the reception desk with its giant bouquet of flowers and glanced around. Everything looked the same as last year. The fans that hung down from the ceiling made a soft *wup-a-wup* sound. Nearby, water splashed in the fountain. She heard a murmur of voices from an alcove off the lobby.

"That you, Maile?" one of the desk clerks asked. She leaned against the gleaming counter. "Philomena will be upset to hear she missed you. Leilani, she'll be sad, too."

Maile nodded. But she couldn't talk about them now.

"We never get to see you." The clerk, who was Philomena's mother, continued. "Too bad Tutu Lady doesn't drive. It must be lonely out in the valley. You get a ride today?"

Maile nodded again, suddenly shy. Of course she'd

had a ride. Mrs. Chong's fish truck was parked by the front entrance. And Tutu Lady waited, as she always did, by the luggage stand up front so she could see.

Maile touched the shiny leaves around her neck. "I've come . . ." she started to say to Philomena's mother. But her voice sounded bumpy. A lump in her throat made it hard to talk. She looked across the lobby at the familiar photograph in the koa-wood frame—a hula dancer, an old-timey picture by some famous photographer. The back of her shoulders tightened.

She turned away from the reception desk and walked across the lobby until she stood in front of the picture. To her, the Hawaiian dancer seemed to beckon. To sway.

"Oh, Maile. Can you reach?" Philomena's mother walked around the reception desk. "Here, let me help you."

"I can reach, thanks."

Standing on tiptoe, Maile stretched her arms high and looped her lei over the picture frame. "*Aloha*," she whispered. "*Aloha nui loa.*" Hawaiian words for love. The dancer was holding her arms open. So close. Maile smiled at her.

And from inside the koa-wood picture frame, surrounded by the shiny green leaves from the forest, her mama smiled back.

## Ratman's Invitation

*O*n the way home from the hotel, Tutu Lady and
Maile sat squeezed together on the front seat of Mrs.
Chong's fish truck, glad for the ride. Only, Mrs. Chong
drove so slowly!

Maile stared out the open window as the truck rumbled through the plantation town. Past old storefronts,
boarded up. Monkeypod trees. Stubble grass and lava
rock walls. Still warmed by Mama's smile, Maile
twirled one of the fern bracelets around her wrist.

As they neared her friend Charlie Wu's house, Maile
leaned out the truck window. Sometimes Charlie hung
around the mill or the post office or the old theater
with the posters on the outside walls. But today, all she
saw were giant sugarcane trucks waiting to be un-

loaded. Everywhere was a sour smell of rotting cane trash. She settled back against the seat. Down the road she could see the school playground with its empty swings, baking in the summer sun.

Her thoughts drifted. They billowed out like a fishnet and caught an awful memory—when some bullies at school had chanted no-good things about her papa. Everyone else had backed away that afternoon. Even Philomena.

"You think your papa's coming back? Ha!"

"What do you know?" Maile had yelled. She hadn't started the fight. No way. But she'd finished it. Maile and Charlie. He'd come to help—shoving his way through the kids, his arms moving like a kung fu man. He'd grinned at her, his glasses all crooked on his face. Afterward, they'd had to sit on the bench outside Mr. Martin's office for cooldown time.

"So your papa left," Charlie had said. "Lotta guys dey *hele* on—they take off." He often spoke pidgin— the words sounded choppy or sometimes almost like music.

Maile had had to turn away. It was hard to be fierce when someone was kind. Because Charlie knew Papa hadn't just left the island—he'd found a whole new family and left Maile behind. More than two years already. Maile had bitten her lip. Maybe those kids had been right. Maybe he wasn't ever coming back.

When Charlie'd said Papa's new wife, Danielle, looked pretty in the photograph Papa sent at Christmas, Maile hadn't talked to Charlie for at least a week.

How could he have said that? And so what! She didn't care about Papa anyhow. Not anymore. She'd fight anybody who said she did.

The fish truck hit a rut, bouncing Maile's daydream away. "I promised Mr. Oshima I'd help today," she said, sneaking her words in between the chatter of Tutu Lady and Mrs. Chong. It sounded funny to say "Mr. Oshima." But Mrs. Chong might not understand that Maile usually called him Ratman.

Mostly Maile rode around in Ratman's old Army jeep while he set rat traps for a public health study. Sometimes, though, she got to fill out the record book: Number of rats trapped by the irrigation ditch, field number 54. The "Yes" or "No" in the "evidence of disease" column. It didn't matter that all the rats looked sleek and healthy. It made her feel important, helping.

"He's counting on me." Maile drummed her fingers on the dash. They'd reached the highway again. A tour bus inched past their truck on the narrow two-lane road, then a long line of tourist rental cars followed the bus.

"If we're too late, you can read the book I bought you at the used book sale," Tutu Lady said.

Maile knew the book Tutu Lady meant. It was so old the pages fell out; they smelled of mildew, too. Reading that book was the last thing Maile wanted to do—even if it was about Hawaiian history, Hawaiian culture.

She wished Mrs. Chong would drive faster, but the fish truck rolled along, slow as ever. Mrs. Chong never

7

seemed to notice all the traffic backed up behind them. They passed the housing development with mainland-style houses, and then suddenly, all around them, for miles and miles, lay fields of sugarcane.

Finally Mrs. Chong pulled off the highway and stopped to let them out. A long line of cars and trucks sped past. Maile and her grandmother climbed down and waved as the fish truck drove away, dripping ice water on the pavement. They walked down the dirt road through the cane fields toward home.

"Better run ahead, Maile. It's all right," Tutu Lady said, smiling.

Maile started off, jogging. It was a good mile at least. And then the plantation fields ended, and the valley began. She saw their tiny wood house, the sun shimmering on its tin roof. Clumps of grass grew in the dirt and gravel driveway. A giant mango tree filled the yard in back, towering over the roof. Plenty shade that tree made. Plenty trash, too. That tree took so much room, you could hardly see the old cars in the field. The ones Papa had always meant to fix. Or use for parts.

There was a flash of brown fur as Poi Dog dashed to greet her. Skinny old dog. He nuzzled her hand as she knelt to hug him. They ran together the rest of the way.

Ratman's jeep was in the drive. "Wait for me!" Maile yelled.

Ratman walked up from the ditch where he checked traps. He waved. "Hop in, Maile." He climbed in the driver's seat.

"We'll be right back," Maile told Poi Dog. She held her hand up, palm down. Poi Dog sat. He wore his forlorn how-can-you-leave-me look.

Smiling, Maile crouched in the back of the jeep on the floor. She pressed her feet against the rat bucket to keep it from falling over as the jeep rattled back down the road. The tails of the dead rats arched over the bucket rim, bobbing and swaying. She waved when she saw Tutu Lady coming toward them.

There weren't any houses around except down another dirt road where Opu Huli Lady lived. Otherwise, it was just Maile, Tutu Lady, and Poi Dog living in the valley. Maile's brother, Keoki, had left the year before, all grown up. An Army man.

It was lonely, just as Philomena's mother had said. Maile didn't complain. Well, maybe to Poi Dog but hardly ever to Tutu Lady. After all, Tutu Lady was all the family Maile had now. She wished their little family could be the way it was when Mama lived there. And Papa. All they had now was an empty spot on the living room wall where Mama's picture used to hang. The picture Papa took when he went away.

Maile had a picture of Keoki in her wallet. She had a picture of Papa, too, only she kept it in the bottom of her bureau drawer, facedown.

The jeep sped up, bouncing over the ruts. "We took one maile lei to the Ohana today. For Mama," Maile said.

Ratman glanced back. "That's a nice thing you do, Maile. Your mama would be proud."

"You think so?" Maile asked, secretly pleased.

"I'm sure of it." Ratman smiled in the rearview mirror. "You know, there's someone you should meet at the manager's house at Hale Nani. When you go there sometime."

Maile peered between the front seats. "Like who?" She hadn't thought of people living there. Not now anyway. Most of the houses on the sugar plantation were gone. Torn down.

"One haole girl, that's who," Ratman said. "A white girl. The manager's niece. I think she's about your age. Eleven or twelve."

Someone her age.

"That's great! When can we go?" Maile asked.

Ratman stopped the jeep by the irrigation ditch and hopped down to check traps. "I told her you might be up," he said, "tomorrow."

"You did?" Maile grinned. She grabbed the record book, jumped down from the jeep, and followed him. "Tell me about her," she begged. "All about her."

"You can find out for yourself," he said, smiling, "when we go there."

## 3

# The Meeting

That night Maile tried to see lights of Hale Nani in the hills. But all she saw was a sky filled with stars. She lay on her bed with Poi Dog curled up on the wood floor beside her. A cool breeze swept down from the hills through the valley. She pulled the sheet up tight and closed her eyes.

It would have helped if Ratman had said even some little thing about this haole girl. Maile switched on the light. On the chair next to the bed lay the book from Tutu Lady. Down the center edge of the pages someone had painted a strip of medicine to kill book worms. Maile ran her fingers across three tiny worm holes. Bump, bump, bump. The binding crackled. *Old Hawaii.*

Where was the part Tutu Lady said she should

read? The Hawaiian way to solve family problems—ho'oponopono. What could Tutu Lady be thinking? Maile didn't have any family problems. She hardly had any family. If the book could tell her how to put one together, that would help. She started to read, skipping the really hard words.

The book slipped. When Maile picked it up, the pages fell open to a section of photographs—pictures inside an ancient burial cave. Probably graves of the alii, the ancient chiefs, she'd read about at school. But who wanted to look at pictures like that when you were alone and it was dark? Maile closed the book fast.

The next day, just before lunch, Tutu Lady sorted the mail. With a sigh, she spread the bills out on the kitchen table. And then she smiled. "Maile, there's a letter for you. From your papa."

Maile picked up the envelope. Her eyes hurt like they did when she tried not to cry. Another letter. It was the kind of envelope Papa always used. "I'll be right back." She ran to her room and shut the door.

"Don't take long, Maile. You have to eat lunch before you go to Hale Nani."

Maile didn't answer. She leaned against the door, holding her letter. Should she open it? Sometimes, when a letter arrived, she almost did. But that would be like saying what Papa had done was okay, and it wasn't. He'd left.

Each time a letter came, she felt this tug-of-war—back and forth.

"Maile, hurry," Tutu Lady called.

In a flash, Maile lifted the end of her mattress. She stuffed the newest letter with the rest of unopened letters, all held together with a rubber band. Then she put the mattress back and smoothed the spread. "Coming." She opened her bedroom door.

Right after lunch, Ratman and Maile left for Hale Nani. When they started up the long drive to the plantation, Ratman turned the wheel hard to avoid the potholes. Then they drove into the parking area in back of the main house. Maile climbed down and threw her thongs, her "slippers," in the jeep. She wiggled her toes in the grass.

"I'll meet you here after I tend traps." Ratman took his bags of coconut meat, wooden traps, and a fresh bucket for dead rats. He moved down into the gulch.

Before Maile was Hale Nani, the beautiful house. The manager's home. One big, fancy place! Two stories even. Yet the wide porches on either side—like open arms—welcomed. Maile took a step closer. A breeze rustled the leaves in the trees. It rippled through her hair as she stood there—a fluttery feeling in her stomach.

A screen door slammed shut, and a girl skipped down the steps. Maile melted into the shadows of the mango tree.

"Hi," the girl said, walking across the grass toward Maile. A wide-brimmed beach hat hid her face. "Mr. Oshima said you might come. My name is Brooke."

Maile stepped out of the shadows and into the sunshine. "I'm Maile Kahona," she said, giving part of her Hawaiian name, not Papa's last name. Brooke didn't need to know her haole name. Not yet, anyway. But it was weird talking to someone when all you could see was her mouth and the tip of her nose.

"Would you like something cool to drink?" Brooke asked.

Maile looked down at her feet, dusty with red dirt. "No, thank you," she said, embarrassed. How could she go inside such a fancy place with dirty feet?

"I guess we could stay outside," Brooke said slowly.

Brooke wore expensive-looking clothes as if she were staying at some fancy resort. Probably that's why she wanted to go inside. So they wouldn't get mussed. Then the brim of Brooke's hat lifted with the breeze. She looked so disappointed. Maybe Maile should've said yes. She opened her mouth to explain about the red dirt, when Brooke's hat blew off. It sailed across the grass.

Maile stared. Brooke was completely bald.

**4**

## Brooke

**B**rooke ran her hands over her bald head. "I look awful, don't I?"

"Nooo," Maile said slowly. Brooke didn't even have eyelashes, but her blue eyes were so beautiful maybe it didn't matter. Her ears looked okay, too. They lay flat. Maile thought of her own ears and felt glad her long hair covered them up.

"I haven't been outdoors for a long time," Brooke said. She talked formally like a teacher—not like a kid at all.

Maile picked up Brooke's hat and gave it to her. "Here," she said. It was hard talking to a person she didn't know. Especially someone who looked as if she'd been left in a washing machine with too much bleach. Brooke really needed to be outside more.

15

Brooke put her hat back on. She peered out from under the brim. "I've been in the hospital," she said. "That's why I'm so white. My hair fell out from the chemotherapy."

Maile's face felt hot. It was almost as if Brooke knew what Maile had been thinking—about how pale she looked.

"I go to school in Seattle, only I missed a lot, because of being sick," Brooke said.

She didn't act angry. Maybe she was used to people who stared even when they didn't mean to.

"Was it . . . cancer?" Maile asked, remembering one of Tutu Lady's friends. Mrs. Olsen had lost all her hair from therapy when she'd had cancer.

Brooke lifted the brim of her hat. "Yes. But I'm all right now. Except, I wish my hair would grow back." She made a face.

"It'll come back," Maile said. The words just popped out, so fast.

"Do you really think so?" Brooke asked, her voice full of hope. "They told me it would. They gave me little pamphlets, even, about what to expect. Only nothing's happened."

Maile nodded, wishing she hadn't said anything. She didn't know anything about getting hair to grow. Could one of the island healers help? Maile had no idea whether or not they specialized in bald heads. Her grandmother knew all about herbs, and Opu Huli Lady massaged stomachs. In ancient times the kahunas, or healers, might have known how to make hair grow.

But what about today? Papa might know. Medical technicians knew everything.

*What if there wasn't anything they could do?* Brooke might have to be bald forever.

Brooke ran up the back steps and wiped her feet on the mat. "Come on, it's hot. Let's get something to drink. Don't worry about the red dirt. I'm always covered with it."

She'd noticed! Maile dusted off her feet. Brooke hung her hat up. Together they walked inside through the two plantation kitchens. There were three refrigerators! How many refrigerators did Hale Nani need, anyway? When Brooke opened the door of the nearest one, Maile peered inside. A cloud of cold air escaped. The cold felt good.

Brooke shut the refrigerator door. "Guava juice." Maile held the glasses as Brooke poured. They gulped down the juice and left the glasses on the counter.

"How long are you going to stay here?" Maile asked.

"A long time. That's what Mother promised me in the hospital when I was so sick." Brooke shoved the dining room door open and walked inside. "I wish you lived closer. Nobody else lives up here."

"Not anymore," Maile said. You could hardly find where the head luna's house used to be. The boss man. Or where the workers had lived when Tutu Lady was a girl—in the plantation camp. Jungle covered everything now.

"Living here isn't anything like Mother's condominium in Seattle."

17

"It isn't like my grandmother's house, either," Maile said. If Brooke only knew!

"Or my father's apartment. It's nice here. Uncle Bill treats me like a regular kid. Not like I'm sick." Brooke darted to the far end of a dining room table that seemed to go on forever. "Let's sit." Leaning to one side, she looked down the length of the table. Maile looked back. She sat, perched on the edge of her chair. Her bare feet sank into the soft rug.

"I like to practice sliding the salt shaker from one end to the other." Brooke grinned. "Like this." The crystal salt shaker zoomed down the table to Maile.

Maile caught the shaker in her hand. "Is this where you eat?" she asked.

"Mostly we eat at the little table over there."

Maile looked at the table against the wall. It looked like one anyone would use, sort of ordinary. If she lived at Hale Nani, she'd practice shooting the salt shaker down the big table, too. And she'd eat at the big table even if it was only her and Tutu Lady. Just for fun.

"There's fresh wax on the living room floor. We can help polish. Want to?" Brooke asked, leading the way past living room chairs and tables crowding the hallways.

Maile edged past the furniture. "Okay," she said, trying to be polite.

The floor stretched out before them. It was huge. They'd be polishing forever. Brooke grabbed some thick dust cloths from a pile on the floor. Standing on the cloths, she skated across the floor. She tossed some cloths to Maile. "Mrs. Kohara, the housekeeper, showed me how. Try it."

It looked easy. Maile stepped on the cloths and slid. She hit a slippery spot. Bam! She slammed into the wall. It wasn't easy at all. She rubbed her toes, her knees, even her forehead.

"Here, I'll show you." Brooke held her arms out and grabbed Maile. For a minute, Maile lurched forward. And then, suddenly, she skated. It was wonderful, zooming around on new wax. Wherever they went, they left a trail of shiny wood.

Brooke sped away on her dust cloths. A jeep horn beeped. She peered out the windows. "Mr. Oshima's ready to go. Whatever does he do with those rats?"

"He tests them to see if they carry disease," Maile answered, stepping off her dust-rag skates. "I help him."

The sun streamed through the window behind Brooke. It made a halo around her head. "He said he'd give me a ride to your house sometime. I mean, if that's okay with you. He says you live in Aloha Valley, the most beautiful place on island—the place where the taro grows."

"He checks the valley traps tomorrow," Maile said.

"Good. I'll come."

Brooke wanted to visit!

Maile tried to imagine Brooke in her fancy clothes riding in the jeep with the dead rats. Or wading barefoot into the thick muddy ooze of the taro pond, to pull up one of the potato-like taro roots. It made her smile. But then she thought of the tiny valley house with the termite holes in the living room wall, and the old cars in the field. Her stomach tightened. Would Brooke still want to be friends when she saw all that?

# 5

## Maile's Home

Maile shoved a load of clothes inside the washing machine on the lanai and set the dials. Then she stepped over Poi Dog to reach the broom. She hurried inside to sweep. Everything should look nice for Brooke.

"Tutu Lady," she said through the screen, "the girl from Hale Nani is coming over today."

Tutu Lady paused as she hung wet clothes by the back door. "That's nice."

"Maybe you'll wear your teeth?" Maile asked. Tutu Lady's teeth rested in a jam jar filled with water on the window ledge. They smiled at Maile from between the ripe papayas.

"Maybe." Tutu Lady lifted the empty clothes basket.

Someone rattled the screen door.

Maile ran barefoot through the house. "I'll get it," she yelled to Tutu Lady. She hadn't heard the jeep. How did Brooke get here already?

But it was Charlie, standing on the front porch.

"How's it?" Maile asked, holding the screen door open.

Charlie shoved his glasses higher on his nose. "I'm hot. My brother's bike is busted. It rides crooked." He kicked off his slippers, the ones with the woven straw matting—the sorry pair with the worn-down heels.

"The whole way out here that bike made me go sideways," Charlie said, walking barefoot past Maile.

"It's you, not the bike, Charlie." Maile grinned. "I'll get you some water." She turned on the faucet and let the water run cold. She raised her voice so Charlie could hear her over the splashing water.

"You want to hike to the waterfall at the end of the valley? Or pick green mangoes?" Charlie asked.

"Another time maybe. A new girl's coming over. Her name is Brooke."

"Who?" Charlie asked, leaning against the kitchen counter.

"The manager's niece at Hale Nani," Maile said. She ran water into a glass for Charlie and then led the way into the living room. He gulped the water, then wiped the back of his hand across his mouth.

Maile lifted stacks of folded laundry. "All these piles of laundry look messy."

"It always looks like this." Charlie sat on the edge of the couch.

Maile frowned. Maybe it would be better if Charlie and Brooke weren't visiting at the same time. And yet she was glad Charlie was there. She could pretend she had people over all the time, pretend it was no big deal.

Maile heard Ratman's jeep roll up, crunching the gravel in the driveway. "She's here!"

Together Maile and Charlie pushed open the screen door and ran down the porch steps. Brooke stood by the edge of the drive, wearing a blue baseball cap. Ratman's jeep had started back down the cane road again.

"She's bald," Maile whispered to Charlie, warning him.

"Yeah, right," Charlie said.

He didn't believe her! It was definitely going to be a problem, having Charlie there. But it was too late now.

Wagging his tail, Poi Dog barked at Brooke.

"Poi Dog," Maile yelled.

"It's okay," Brooke said. "I like dogs." She ran her fingers through his coat and smoothed his ears.

"This is Charlie Wu," Maile said as they walked across the yard to the porch.

Charlie straightened his glasses. "Maile tells me you're bald." He laughed. "What a goofball she is."

Maile's face felt hot.

But Brooke giggled. "I *am* bald." She slipped her cap off and stood there in the sunshine.

Charlie's eyes grew big. He pushed up his glasses.

"Oh, wow." He shook his head. "Hey, I didn't know. Maile and me, we clown around a lot."

"It's all right." Brooke's face had turned pink. "I had chemotherapy, that's why."

"Come on inside." Maile hurried up the steps and held the screen door open. She hoped Brooke wouldn't look too carefully at the house. Maybe she could distract her somehow, so Brooke wouldn't notice how shabby everything was. "Guess what? I got an idea for getting your hair to grow, Brooke."

"Really?" Brooke asked.

Maile looked around quickly. She picked up a bowl from the kitchen counter. "Poi. It's a paste made from cooked taro root."

"Since when can poi grow hair?" Charlie asked.

"It's healthy. They even serve it in the hospital." Maile lifted the towel off the bowl so Brooke could smell the poi. Brooke sniffed and drew back.

"That's sour poi," Charlie said. "It's fermented. Some people like it better that way after it's been left out for a day or two."

"It's my grandmother, Tutu Lady's favorite." Maile covered the thick purple-gray mixture with the towel. "But for you, I'll mix a fresh batch, Brooke."

Brooke stared at the poi bowl. "What's it taste like?"

"It's like smooth oatmeal without any sugar," Maile said finally. "But it has more flavor."

Brooke frowned.

"It tastes good," Maile said. "Really, it does."

Charlie grinned. "It's gooey."

You'd think poi was something terrible from the expression on Brooke's face.

"You can eat it like a snack. Or with lunch or dinner. Even breakfast. You'll see," Maile said.

Charlie pulled a cellophane bag from his pocket. "You'll like these better."

"What's that?" Brooke asked suspiciously.

"Crack seed. Here, have some." Charlie squeezed out a lump of sticky preserved fruit and seed for Brooke and one for Maile. "It's Chinese preserved plum. It'll work better than that poi. Taste better, too."

"No way." Maile popped the crack seed into her mouth. Charlie was trying to horn in on her idea. Crack seed couldn't be that healthy. It was salty. She folded her arms. "Poi stops colic in babies. You can use it lots of ways—for scorpion bites, bee stings, skin problems. Paste." She couldn't remember any more of the things she'd learned from Tutu Lady. "And just maybe, it'll work for bald-headed kids." She smiled.

"If you paste the hair on," Charlie said.

That wasn't even funny, Maile thought.

But Brooke didn't seem to pay any attention to what Charlie said. She crunched down on the sticky seeds and pursed her lips. "This tastes good but it's hard to eat."

"I'll teach you how to spit seed," Charlie told her.

Brooke tried to talk as she swallowed bits of preserved plum, then wiped her mouth. "I already know how to spit." The seed shot out of her mouth and hit

25

Charlie right on the neck. She smiled. "It's my aim that's bad."

Charlie grinned. Then he showed Brooke the best place on the couch to sit, the place he usually grabbed first—the cushion that still had springs. As if it were his house and Brooke were his guest!

# The Misfit Club

et's go outside." Maile ran out of the living room onto the porch. "Come on!" She hopped down the porch steps, two at a time. "I'll show you something great, Brooke."

Brooke and Charlie chased after her, leaping off the porch together. Dashing across the grass, Maile led them to the field of tangled vines. There, under the shade of a coconut palm, sat two old cars, stripped of parts.

"Is this part of your yard?" Brooke asked, frowning.

Maile's face grew hot. "It's our field," she said. It was almost as if Brooke had said the field looked like a dump. And it didn't. There wasn't any garbage around—just two old cars that were perfect for sitting in on a hot afternoon.

"The place for the imu, the underground oven, is over there." Maile pointed to the large flat rocks where Charlie stood. There was a hollowed-out place in the dirt.

"Maile's brother cooks kalua pig here," Charlie said. "He digs out the pit, heats up the rocks, and puts the pig in the ground to cook. Everybody helps. It's a lotta work."

"A whole pig?" Brooke teetered on top of the rock pile. "How terrible."

How did Brooke think you cooked a pig, anyway? In pieces? Maile lifted a morning-glory vine off the door of the nearest car and climbed in the front seat with Poi Dog.

"I've always wanted a pig for a pet," Brooke told Charlie. "I could never eat one."

Charlie took his glasses off and polished them with his T-shirt. "I like pigs, too. They're intelligent."

Maile almost fell out of the car. "Sure you like pigs. You eat them all the time!" The Charlie she knew seemed to be changing right before her eyes. Worse, he didn't seem to notice her at all anymore.

"Most people think kalua pig is a treat," Maile continued. Brooke made cooking a pig sound like something bad. What did she know?

Brooke fanned herself with her cap. When Charlie climbed in the backseat of Maile's car, she slipped her baseball cap back on and sat beside him.

She could've sat in front with Poi Dog and Maile. Who'd Brooke come to visit anyway?

"I could teach you how to drive, Brooke." Maile looked at Brooke in the rearview mirror. "My brother taught me in his jeep. I've gone all around the field. Even down the cane road. Of course, it won't be real driving, not in an old car without any insides."

But Brooke didn't answer. Instead, she screamed.

Maile spun around. "What?"

Brooke tumbled out of the car. "A spider! It's this big . . ." She held her fingers and thumb apart as wide as they could go.

Charlie laughed. "It's just a cane spider. He won't hurt you. My brother keeps one as a pet." Still, Charlie crouched up on the seat, ready to jump.

"It disappeared," Brooke whispered, "under the seat."

Maybe it was crawling up front. Maile jerked her feet off the floor. With a shudder, she leaped from the car. "Come on," she yelled, pulling Brooke away.

They ran without looking back, Poi Dog and Charlie at their heels. Tutu Lady held the screen door open as the three of them burst into the house. They squeezed onto the couch, breathing hard. Outside, Poi Dog whined at the door.

"Hello, Charlie," Tutu Lady said. Her teeth gleamed when she smiled. "And you must be Maile's friend from Hale Nani."

Brooke slid off the couch. "I'm Brooke," she said.

She looked so formal, shaking Tutu Lady's hand.

"Are you thirsty?" Tutu Lady asked Brooke. The two of them walked to the refrigerator, chatting together as if they were old friends. Tutu Lady poured passion fruit juice into four jelly glasses.

"I just mixed some fresh poi," Tutu Lady told Brooke. "Have you ever tried it?"

"I'd like a small taste. A very small taste," Brooke answered, lifting her cap off and shoving it in her back pocket. She glanced at Maile and winked. "Maybe it will help my hair grow. I get tired of wearing hats, and I hate wearing my wig. It's too hot."

That Brooke was okay. Maile grinned.

"It's the same with my false teeth," Tutu Lady admitted. "They fit too tight. They hurt." Brooke and Tutu Lady laughed.

"Right on," Charlie said, joining them at the sink. He took his thick glasses off. "I hate wearing my glasses all the time. They're too heavy."

Maile never knew Charlie didn't like his glasses. She'd never thought about them being heavy. They made him look brainy, even handsome. They all seemed glad to have something that didn't fit. Like they belonged to some secret club—a misfit club. Well, Maile had something that didn't fit, too. Herself. She felt left out.

Tutu Lady handed out glasses of juice. She put four small bowls of poi on the table. She showed Brooke how to swirl the poi up from the bowl with a twist of her fingers. Brooke closed her eyes as she ate. She scrunched her mouth and eyes in a grimace. Charlie's eyes twinkled. Tutu Lady and Maile started to smile. Each time Brooke swallowed, she made an awful face. Almost like poi was some kind of medicine.

Maybe it was! The more Maile thought how poi might help Brooke's hair grow, the more convinced she became. She'd ask Ratman to help—she'd send a big batch of fresh poi to Hale Nani every day. The more the better. A soupy three-finger poi. And the next day, two-finger poi. And then, the day after that, she'd send the real thick stuff, one-finger poi. Brooke might even learn to like it.

## Little Beach

The next day, Maile hitched a ride with Ratman to the little plantation office building. Ratman drove into the parking area, which was almost empty, gathered his papers, and climbed out of the jeep.

"I'll be down by Charlie's house," Maile said.

Ratman had started down the sidewalk to the office. He turned. "They went fishing today. Early this morning."

"Oh." Maile tried to keep the disappointment out of her voice. Charlie was the real reason she'd come. "I guess I'll go down to Little Beach then."

From across the road, the sugar mill belched clouds of steam. Giant cane trucks rumbled past. So noisy. There was a loud, piercing sound of air escaping the big tanks inside the mill. She darted away from the mill yard and down the crooked street past Charlie's empty house to the skinny strip of beach that ran for miles along the water's edge. Standing on the beach, she stared out at the water.

"My-lee!" It was Brooke, holding her hat on her head as she ran. "Ratman told me you might be here." She took off her sandals and plowed across the sand. Her hat flew off. She lurched forward, snatching it mid-air. "This crazy hat."

Brooke looked so funny. Maile grinned. Gosh, her head looked shiny. It reminded Maile to ask Ratman to take poi to Hale Nani. The sooner, the better, she thought. Brooke needed all the help she could get. Maile scooped up a handful of sand and let it trickle through her fingers. "You come with your uncle?"

Brooke nodded, smiling.

"That's Charlie's house over there." Maile pointed back down the road. "Only, he's not home."

"I knew he lived around here somewhere," Brooke said. "But his house looks nice. One of the workers said a tidal wave washed it away. I think he was kidding me."

"No, he wasn't," Maile said. "It happened a long time ago. Charlie's folks, they fixed the place up." She hopped in the sand, first on one foot, then on the other. The sand was hot. She waded into the water. "The ocean is like a big bathtub today."

Brooke followed. She splashed water on her arms

and then looked back at Charlie's house. "It doesn't look like anything happened to his house."

"Oh, it's true, all right. They found his house in the gulch. The refrigerator, too. The crane lifted up the house and sand poured out the doors. Seashells rattled around inside. They set it down right there, where it used to be."

"But couldn't another wave come? In the same place?" Brooke asked.

"Yes." Maile shielded her eyes. The ocean looked smooth, almost flat. It reminded her of the story Tutu Lady told about that very same day. The memory made her knees weak. She stepped out of the water and sat on the sand. "Other things happened then, too. Sad things."

"I know the Ohana Hotel got wiped out and had to be rebuilt. Mother took me there for breakfast. I read the wall plaque, but mostly it's just a list of names." Brooke sat down in the sand next to Maile. "What happened?"

Maile wrapped her arms around her legs. "You sure you want to hear? It's sad."

"Sure, I'm sure," Brooke said.

"There were lots of false alarms that summer," Maile began. "I was three years old, just a little kid. But folks said there was an earthquake in some faraway place, and the civil defense sirens would warn everyone of possible tsunamis, tidal waves. Over and over again. Only, the waves never came. So when the sirens sounded that day, no one believed. Besides, the ocean looked shiny and soft. The way it looks now, today."

Brooke sat up, her eyes wide. "Oh." She looked out at the ocean and then back at Maile.

Maile's chest tightened. "You really want to hear this story?" Her heart started to pound.

"Yes. Don't stop now."

"The siren sounded again, a second time. Then the water started going out to sea, real fast. Like a big low tide. Only it went out farther than anyone had ever seen. Children ran to see the pretty shells. Where people used to drop anchor, fish flopped on the wet sand. Their scales sparkled in the sun like little rainbows. Folks picked up fish for supper. Tourists grabbed their cameras. No one thought of danger. They'd heard all those false alarms. One by one, they ran out farther and farther."

Maile took a deep breath. "But a Hawaiian dancer at the Ohana Hotel saw the way the ocean looked. She knew what it meant. My mama. She tried to warn everybody. To save them. She ran across the wet sand. . . ." Maile tried to tell the story the way Tutu Lady did. Only it was hard to talk. She imagined her mama running and running and the sirens wailing.

Maile took another deep breath. Her arms tightened around her knees. "The ocean coiled back like a big snake, the water turning dark green, then black. It roared. The first giant wave hurled itself against the beach. Auwe!"

"And your mama?" Brooke asked.

35

"She died," Maile said. Then she added what Tutu Lady always did. "So good and brave she was." Because it was true.

"I'm so sorry," Brooke said.

"Her picture is at the Ohana Hotel, in the lobby," Maile said.

## Wu's Place

**E**arly the next morning, Maile washed her hands. Twice. Then she squeezed the cooked, mashed taro root between her fingers, mixing it with water. Gooey library paste—that's what it looked like. She grinned, picturing Brooke with hair sprouts all over her head.

Ratman had promised to deliver the poi to Hale Nani every day. He was such a good friend to agree. He helped her out a lot. When he picked the poi up, Maile wedged the bowl in a box so it wouldn't tip over. "Hey, thanks," she said.

It was an exciting project. Maile zoomed around the house, happy she'd sent the poi to Brooke. She offered to help Tutu Lady weed the taro pond out back. She stood in the muck, watching how the light sparkled on

37

the water, how the big taro leaves, like giant Valentine hearts, bowed to one another in the breeze. Sometimes she found a weed and pulled it.

Maile remembered Brooke's expression after her first taste of poi. All the faces she'd made. Even knowing that poi might help! Maile could hardly wait till Brooke called to say thank you. Or hello. Or that was quite a story you told me about your mama, Maile. Thank you for sharing. She wondered if Brooke knew that was the first time Maile ever told it. To anyone.

They were going to be friends, Maile could tell. Brooke even knew what it was like when your papa left. Or when your mother wasn't around. They had a lot in common.

The phone didn't ring until after supper. By then Maile and Poi Dog lay sprawled in front of the TV. Maile was half asleep. "I'll get it!" Maile yelled, rubbing her eyes. She ran to the phone. "Hi," she said into the receiver. Suddenly she couldn't remember all the important things she'd saved up to say. "Brooke?"

"Eh, that you Maile? You and Tutu Lady want lau-lau tickets? Church benefit," Mrs. Chong said.

Oh, no! Mrs. Chong would tie up the phone line. Maile handed the receiver to Tutu Lady. They talked a long, long time.

The phone didn't ring again that night.

It rained hard the next day. Maile waited on the porch with the poi bowl on her lap. Finally the jeep drove through the cane fields. "Sorry I'm late," Ratman said. "The rain washed away part of the road." Little rivers of water ran down his hat. "But I'll get this up to Hale Nani. No problem."

"How did Brooke look yesterday?" Maile asked from the porch.

"Fine," Ratman said.

"You didn't notice anything different about her?" Maile asked. Brooke's hair must not have started to grow yet. At least not so that it showed. Maybe overnight was expecting too much.

Ratman shook his head. "Hey, later." The jeep splashed through giant puddles in the dirt road. Maile sat back down on the porch.

It rained harder. The yard began to look like a small pond. Even Poi Dog stayed on the porch. But by late afternoon, when the sun came out again, the yard dried up. Everything looked as it usually did. Still, if Brooke was eating poi and growing new hair, she wasn't sharing the news with Maile. Maybe something was wrong. Besides, there were so many things they could do. Like go to the beach or hike. Even visit Charlie.

Maile dialed the Hale Nani number and let it ring and ring. Twice she called.

The next day she tried again. A busy signal! Two, three more times she tried. Nothing. No one answered. Maybe they'd all gone to the grocery store together. Or to the beach.

"Ratman, what does Brooke say when you take her the poi?" Maile asked.

"She says thank you." Ratman looked away when he answered. "There's company at Hale Nani now."

"Oh!" That explained it. Brooke was too busy to call. They were probably seeing the sights, eating out. When Maile mixed the next batch of poi, she hummed along with a song on the radio. Suddenly she held the spoon up. Could anybody be that busy? Wouldn't a friend at least try to call?

In the afternoon, as they usually did, Maile and Poi Dog sat in the old car together. That day she took the book Tutu Lady bought her and flipped through the pages. Tutu Lady had said to read the part about ho'oponopono: How to mend a family. How to make things right. If only a book could . . . maybe she could even make things right with Papa.

Tutu Lady carried lemonade out to Maile. "Let's talk story," Tutu Lady said.

Maile and Poi Dog made room for her on the front seat of the old car. Maile leaned back, soaking in the warm sun. She sipped her lemonade. "Tell me about the time you met the shark out on the reef." She loved that story.

"How about one story about family? About Papa?" Tutu Lady asked. "Wouldn't it be nice if he came to visit?"

"Talk story today? Now?" Suddenly Maile's stomach had an ache. Maybe she'd drunk the lemonade too fast.

"I don't feel so good. Maybe we can talk story later," she said.

Tutu Lady looked thoughtfully at Maile. "Okay, another time. I've got plenty work to do." She took Maile's empty lemonade glass and walked back to the house.

As soon as Tutu Lady disappeared inside the house, Maile stood up. Already her stomach felt better.

A week went by without a word from Brooke. At least Charlie called. "I'm sending poi to Hale Nani," Maile told him.

"Poi won't make her hair grow, Maile," Charlie said.

"It might. You don't know. Anyway, it can't hurt."

"You should send poi to our restaurant. At least we'd pay for it. Or send some to me. I love it."

Maile giggled.

She didn't sing with the radio when she mixed poi, as she usually did. She didn't even bother to turn the radio on. Instead, she dialed Philomena's number, just to talk. "Philomena's visiting her cousins on the mainland, Maile. I'll tell her you called," her mother said.

"Yeah, thanks, eh?" Maile hung the receiver up. On Tuesday she called Leilani.

"Humbug this summer," Leilani said. "I have to baby-sit every day."

For some reason, knowing that about Leilani made Maile feel better. Still, the next day, Maile shoved the bowl away. It wasn't fun anymore mixing poi. How busy could Brooke be? Not to make one telephone call, one small thank you? She could mix her own poi!

When Ratman arrived, Maile shook her head. "I'm not sending any poi," she said, her voice low. "Not anymore."

Ratman seemed to understand. When his jeep disappeared down the cane road, Maile leaned against the screen door for a long time.

Wednesday night Tutu Lady's friend, Aunty Abigail, drove Maile to get Chinese take-out food for Tutu Lady's quilting group. Maile lugged cooking pots up the rickety old steps to Wu's restaurant. She hoped Charlie would be there. Inside, she lifted the pots up on the counter and waited to give her order to fill them.

The light in the foyer swayed in the breeze, flickering dim and yellow. Maile leaned against the counter. Suddenly the kitchen door swung open and Charlie appeared. Maile smiled. "You look great!" He wore a big white apron wrapped around his middle, like a professional chef.

"Thanks." Charlie lifted the pots she brought off the counter. "Long time no see."

"What's happening?" Maile asked, just like old times.

"You see Brooke?" Charlie asked.

Didn't he think of anything else besides Brooke? "No," Maile said shortly.

Charlie laughed. Maile didn't think it was funny. But when Charlie laughed, it was hard not to smile.

"You kidding me?" Charlie asked.

"No. What do you mean?"

Charlie started to back into the swinging door. He pointed toward the dining room. "She's in there."

Maile's heart jumped when she saw the backward baseball cap. Brooke sat next to her uncle and across the table was a lady with blond hair. How could she get away before Brooke saw her?

"Is our food almost ready?" the blond lady asked loudly when Charlie returned.

Charlie nodded. Ducking below the counter, Maile edged away from the dining room.

"Maile," Brooke called out. She shoved her chair back. "I didn't know you were here. Come meet my mother. She's visiting at Hale Nani."

Maile took a few steps toward the table.

"Hello," the blond lady said.

Maile turned toward her. "Hello." But Maile really wanted to talk to Brooke, to say How come you so rude, Brooke? Never calling? Instead, she looked down at the floor.

"Maile lives in the valley," Brooke told her mother. She slipped off her cap and turned to Maile. "The poi didn't work."

"Well, we tried," Maile said, pretending she wasn't surprised.

"Right," Brooke said.

"Put your hat on, Brooke," her mother said, looking around to see if anyone was watching.

Brooke eased her baseball cap back on. She pulled it low. How cross Brooke's mother sounded. Maile almost made an island shaka sign to Brooke. A hang-in-there kind of sign. She stopped herself. Brooke didn't care about the poi. She didn't even say thank you. She probably wouldn't care about a shaka sign either.

"Maile, your order's on the counter," Charlie said as he set food on the table for Brooke's family.

"Nice to meet you," Maile said, backing away. At last she could go. She lifted the pots off the counter, slipped outside, and hurried down the path to Aunty Abigail's car.

# 9

## Ho'oponopono

### How to Make Things Right Again

**B**rooke called the very next morning as if nothing was wrong. "I'm going away," she said. Wasn't Brooke going to say she was sorry?

"How long will you be gone?" Maile asked.

"A few days," Brooke answered.

"Well, have a good time." Maile hung up. She pushed the screen door open to sit down on the porch steps. Tutu Lady was spading dirt around a clump of flowers in the garden.

"Brooke's going off island." Maile stared at the grass.

"She just got here," Tutu Lady said. "I wonder why she has to go now? You think anything is wrong?"

Maile shrugged. What did she care? Brooke could

stay off island. Forever. For the rest of the day, Maile helped Tutu Lady work in the garden. In bed that night, she read some more in the book Tutu Lady had given her: *Old Hawaii*. The part about ho'oponopono. She sounded out each vowel: hoe-oh-poh-no-poh-no. The book was hard to read! Such long words. She had to read some parts two, even three times. She kept hunting for some little clue that might help fix things between her and Papa. She was going to forget Brooke. Who needed her?

*When a family has problems and wants to make things right again—you need a mediator to hear things out. To keep things fair.* Sort of like a referee, Maile thought. That sounded okay.

*You can't be angry when you talk to the other person.* Who were they kidding? She closed the book around her finger.

What she needed was something easy to use like a recipe anyone could follow: How to mend your family. How to keep your friends. Like an offer on TV. Send money, results guaranteed. Instant cure.

Maile flipped back to the section about ho'opono-pono. At the end of one of the pages was something she hadn't read before. It made the back of her neck feel cold. *Failing to forgive is one of the worst offenses.* There was a list of things that could happen. None of them good. Well, it couldn't mean her. She was just a kid.

Maile slipped out of bed and ran barefoot into the

living room. Tutu Lady sat on the couch, her crochet hook flashing in the light.

"I read some of that book you gave me, the part about ho'oponopono." Maile curled up next to Tutu Lady on the couch. "If you talk story, it would be better. That book is hard to understand."

"I didn't think you wanted to talk story anymore."

"This is different," Maile said.

Tutu Lady laid down her crochet work and smiled at Maile. "Once," she began, "a Hawaiian family lived in a small house next to a mango tree. So big that tree! And the fruit was ono ono—so extra delicious that they picked it green.

"Only mangoes on the top branches were there long enough to get ripe. When the ripe fruit fell down, the keikis, the children, gathered mangoes so their mama could make chutney and mango bread to sell."

Maile's mouth watered. She loved mango bread, warm from the oven.

"But first those kids tasted the ripe mangoes. So sweet and juicy. When they went inside, they called, 'Mama, no more mangoes.' They'd eaten every last one.

" 'What you think?' Mama yelled. 'Eating all those mangoes!' She say plenty things to those kids. None of them nice.

"And the kids say plenty things back. The oldest child, a boy, glared at his mama. 'I no like the way you talk.'

" 'I only ate two mangoes,' his little sister said. 'I not sorry.'

"When the papa got home, everyone was saying mean things. Nothing was ready for supper, and the family went to bed hungry.

"The next morning, things weren't any better.

"Auwe! Everyone was so unhappy!

" 'That tree make plenty trouble,' Papa said. 'If I chop it down, you can't fight about it anymore.'

"But the young daughter, who was very wise, said, 'Papa, it's not the tree. It's all of us.'

"Everyone agreed. It wasn't the tree. They glared at each other again.

"After breakfast the daughter said they should try ho'oponopono, to set things right. Papa offered to lead.

" 'Sounds good,' Mama said.

" 'We might even invite Uncle here, to mediate,' the daughter suggested.

"And even though, for small problems, they could solve things themselves, they agreed. Uncle did, too. He arrived that afternoon.

"First, they prayed together. Then each one talked—but no more angry stuff. The children said they didn't mean to eat all the mangoes. Such shame they felt. So sorry, too, about the mean kind of things they'd said to Mama.

" 'I didn't mean to be so cross,' Mama said, sniffling.

"Papa said he didn't really want to chop down the mango tree.

"They forgave each other. One by one. They gave thanks. That mango problem was pau. All done. They set themselves free of it. And by and by they made a meal to eat together—to celebrate."

"What they did sounds easy," Maile said.

"The hardest part," Tutu Lady said, "was for them to listen to each other and not argue. To forgive."

Maile nodded. Maybe it wasn't so easy after all.

In her bedroom, Maile turned off the light. She listened to Poi Dog snore. Then she heard a soft thud in the yard outside. A mango falling from the tree. Maile wiggled her toes under the sheet. Slowly she moved her legs along the foot of the bed, her feet searching for a small lump under the mattress, the packet of letters she'd saved from Papa. The mattress felt smooth. She reached down and felt with her fingers. Nothing. She froze. Where were the letters?

# 10

## Keoki

**M**aile scrambled out of bed and turned on the light. The mattress was so thin, the end rolled up easily.

Hadn't she checked Papa's letters when she put the latest letter there? Where were they? Swallowing hard, she shoved the end of the mattress off the springs.

And there, caught between the metal coils, she saw the letters so flat that they looked as if someone had ironed them together.

Maile pulled the packet free and hugged it. Then she shoved the mattress back. What if they'd disappeared? Slowly she worked an envelope out from under the rubber band, from the bottom of the pile. She stopped. It was safer not to open it. She laid the envelope on top of the spread. But it was two years old. What harm could it do?

Poi Dog stretched. He leaned against the bed as Maile tore the envelope open. She pulled out a piece of wrinkled paper and started to read.

*Dear Maile,*

*So, how are you and Keoki-boy? I took that exam. The hospital here is one of the best in California for emergency medical training. I'll let you know how I did. I miss you.*

*Love from your papa.*

Maile read it again. And again. Then she buried her face in the pillow.

Brooke had been gone two days. Not that it made any difference, Maile thought. Except, it was a good time to visit Charlie when Brooke wasn't around. Maile set out, walking along the cane road, Poi Dog at her heels. After a while, Poi Dog pranced on ahead, but suddenly he stopped and sniffed. Maile inhaled, too. The air smelled sweet, like molasses. All around them, black flakes tumbled and fell, sounding like raindrops bouncing on banana leaves as they landed on the ground.

Maile balanced a piece of burnt cane leaf on the palm of her hand and blew it back into the air. She brushed another piece off her T-shirt, leaving a long black smudge. From a slope on the hillside, smoke billowed upward, pumping clouds of gray into the blue sky. The plantation was burning cane for harvest. Even from here, she could hear the crackle of the leaves as they burned. Soon all that would be standing would be the blackened stalks, filled with sugar.

She wondered what Brooke would think of black snow. If she were here, that is. Oh, wow! The laundry! Maile knew what Tutu Lady would think, especially with all the clothes hung out to dry. Maile turned and ran for home. Poi Dog loped ahead, down the cane road, down the drive, across the yard.

Maile yanked towels off the line and threw them over her arm. Clothespins flew to the ground. Tutu Lady carried a pile of laundry in the house. Her voice, trapped inside a pile of sheets, sounded muffled. "It's good you came back."

Maile followed Tutu Lady. "I saw the fire from the road." She started to fold the laundry, inspecting it for black streaks.

"Your brother called from the mainland." Tutu Lady shook one of Maile's shirts. "He's coming to visit."

"When?" Maile asked.

Tutu Lady laughed. "That Keoki! He never gives us much warning. He comes this afternoon."

Maile's heart raced. It seemed like Keoki had been gone forever. "Maybe we can have a luau. Oh, Tutu Lady, how long will the Army let him stay?"

Tutu Lady shook her head. "He didn't say, Maile."

Their rickety house was like an accordion whenever Keoki was around. It expanded as more and more people arrived to see him.

Maile hopped around the living room. Having everyone around with Keoki, they'd be like a big family. It would be wonderful.

"Maybe you and Charlie can make some leis, to welcome Keoki home."

"We'll make plenty leis," Maile said.

Tutu Lady turned. "Ratman's picking me up at two o'clock to meet Keoki's plane. We'll stop at Charlie's place for you."

Maile and Poi Dog ran back down the cane road. Gradually the ashes stopped falling. Slowing to a walk, Maile skimmed pebbles along the top of the irrigation ditch. Papa should be here for the luau, too.

She imagined all the fun things they could do with Keoki home. They'd have kalua pig. Maile's mouth watered just thinking about it. It was better Brooke was off island—loving pigs like she did.

Maile wound her way through the fields, peeking at the blue sky through the towering cane tassels. Ahead, the paved road lay hot in the sun. Giant cane trucks rushed past, spilling stalks. Maile walked faster. An empty cane truck rattled by. After it passed, Maile and Poi Dog darted across the road. They walked and walked, taking shortcuts through the fields. Finally, they ran toward the sugar mill and down the crooked street where Charlie lived. Charlie was sitting on the front steps, a stack of magazines by his side.

"Keoki's coming home today! Let's make him some leis," Maile yelled.

Charlie grinned as he stood up. "It's about time he came back." He walked to the shed and shoved the door open. In a minute he walked out carrying a long bamboo ladder. "I'll hold the ladder." Charlie leaned it against the trunk of a small plumeria tree covered with yellow flowers edged in white.

Maile climbed up the ladder and balanced on the middle rungs. When she stretched, she could just reach the clusters of flowers that grew at the tip of each branch.

"Here's the bucket," Charlie said, handing it up.

Maile slung the handle over her arm. She plucked the velvety blossoms and dropped them into the bucket. White sap stuck to her hands and made sticky glue balls on her fingers. "I'm climbing down." She edged her feet from rung to rung.

Standing by the smaller plumeria trees in back, Maile and Charlie picked pink blossoms from one tree and then some yellow flowers from another. Maile swung the bucket. "Plenty flowers we have." She pushed her hair from her face, careful not to touch her eyes with the milky sap.

Charlie ran inside to find some long needles and strong thread. Then Charlie and Maile sat together in the shade, stringing flowers. Poi Dog yawned. He lay down by Maile's feet and went to sleep.

"So, is Brooke eating poi?" Charlie asked.

"I don't know. She went off island somewhere." Maile jerked her needle through the blossoms and stabbed herself. She squeezed her finger, making it bleed. Brooke was the last person she wanted to talk about.

Maile studied the leis spread out on the grass. Half of them looked too short. Her hands and clothes smelled sickly sweet, like too much perfume. But the leis looked beautiful.

"I wonder if Brooke went for a cancer checkup," Charlie said.

"Her cancer's all gone," Maile said.

"Yeah, but they still check, in case it comes back."

"How do you know?" Maile asked, frowning.

"My uncle told us his cancer was gone. Only it popped up again," Charlie said.

Maile stared. She'd never thought of that. The idea of Brooke's cancer coming back made her stomach feel like waves were rolling inside. Maybe she should've been nicer to Brooke when she called. What if Charlie was right?

When Ratman and Tutu Lady arrived on their way to the airport, Maile, Charlie, and Poi Dog climbed in the back of the jeep. Maile piled the leis on the seat. The jeep roared. Off they went, bouncing over the beach road. Up in front, Tutu Lady clutched her hat, the one with the feather lei. Her muumuu billowed in the wind.

On they sped, past a tour bus and a line of cars on the winding road, past the beach hotels and the time-share condominiums. Poi Dog's nose quivered. The smell of salt ponds mingled with the plumeria perfume and diesel fumes.

"The flight's here," Ratman said as they careened around the road. The jeep bounced. Maile tumbled into the flowers. Ratman shifted down. Parked on the small interisland runway, a silvery plane glittered between palm fronds.

As soon as the jeep stopped, Charlie and Maile leaped out. She slung the leis over her arms and ran. Poi Dog reached the wire gate first, then Maile.

Keoki walked down the plane ramp. So rugged and handsome. Maile jumped and waved. "Keoki!" she yelled, her voice into the wind.

Someone next to Maile brushed against the flowers. "I'm glad Keoki's finally coming home."

Maile turned. What was Keoki's old girlfriend doing here?

"Oh, hi, Rosemary," she said.

Rosemary smiled, her lipstick glossy, her teeth bright white. Maile burst past her, through the gate. But Rosemary ran faster. Right up to Keoki! When she hugged him, there wasn't any room left for Maile.

Maile looked past them, to the plane. Someone was walking down the ramp, all alone. Someone small and bald.

## 11

# Home Again

It had to be Brooke walking toward them. Maile tried to peek around Rosemary and Keoki. Suddenly Maile was wrapped in Keoki's arms. She slipped the flower leis over his neck, one by one. "Welcome home, Keoki," she said softly.

"Good to see you." Keoki mussed her hair. "Thanks, eh, for all the leis. Hey, there's someone I want you to meet, Maile. Someone I met on the plane."

Keoki always had someone to introduce. But it was Brooke this time!

"We know each other already," Maile said.

"Hi, Maile," Brooke said, putting her hat back on. It was a new hat with a velvet ribbon. Everything she wore looked crisp and new.

"Hi." Maile shifted, uncomfortable. She looked at her own sun-faded T-shirt and shorts, her rubber-thong sandals.

"So you're already friends." Keoki laughed. "Two little seestahs," he said, saying "sisters" the pidgin way. He put an arm around Rosemary. "Meet you two at the gate."

"Sure," Maile said, sneaking another look at Brooke. They started to walk across the tarmac together.

Brooke twisted the ribbon on her hat. "There's something I need to tell you, Maile." She looked at the ground. "I never ate the poi. I was trying to forget about being bald. About cancer. And every day there was that gooey stuff I was supposed to eat. It made me gag. I'm sorry."

"You could've told me. I was just trying to kokua, to help."

"I know." There was a long pause. They kept on walking, side by side. "My mother stayed at Hale Nani all this past week." Brooke's voice sounded low, almost like a whisper. "She doesn't want me to talk pidgin."

"I didn't know you did," Maile said.

"Well, I'm trying. But Mother doesn't like it."

"Some of my teachers are like that," Maile said. "They think it's bad English."

"But Mother . . . oh, Maile, she doesn't want me to be with anyone who does."

"But your uncle Bill talks pidgin. Island people do." Maile turned and stared at Brooke. Her face felt hot.

"Doesn't she know we speak regular American English, too?"

"Yes," Brooke said.

"That's why you didn't call, isn't it? That's the real reason," Maile said. "She think I'm not good enough?"

"She doesn't know how wonderful everyone is here. That you and I are friends. If she could be here longer, she'd find out what the island is really like."

Maile wasn't so sure. Brooke's mother sounded mean and cross. Probably she'd have to be on island for a very long time for it to make any difference. To make her nice. Something like that wouldn't happen overnight. But Maile didn't want to discourage Brooke. After all, it was her mother.

Brooke took her hat off. "And I should've eaten the poi, Maile. My hair hasn't grown at all. I look terrible."

"You don't look so bad. Your ears are nice and flat. Now if I was bald, it would be a disaster." Maile held her hair up. "My ears stick out." She couldn't believe she was showing Brooke her ears.

"They don't stick out much."

Maile let her hair fall back down. "Really?"

"I bet nobody notices your ears. But people stare at me."

"Some people have no manners," Maile said. "Make stink eye. Geev'em one dirty look. I do."

Brooke smiled. "Yeah. That's what I'll do, too."

They rode home together with Poi Dog and Charlie in the plantation car. Brooke's uncle drove. Maile waved as Ratman's jeep drove past. "See you soon," she yelled to Keoki, who cuddled next to Rosemary in the back of Ratman's jeep.

"So where were you, Brooke?" Maile asked as Poi Dog settled beside her. "The mainland?"

"And where's your mother?" Charlie chimed in.

"I went to a hospital on Oahu," Brooke said, "for my cancer checkup." Then she leaned toward Charlie. "And my mother has a new modeling assignment. She couldn't come back to Hale Nani now. She travels a lot with her job."

"You told me the cancer was gone," Maile said, frowning.

"It was gone. And they didn't find any this time either."

*This time*, Maile thought. The words stuck in her head. What about next time?

"Do they think your hair's ever going to grow?" Charlie asked.

Brooke shrugged. "I hope so. I told Dr. Tom about the poi cure. He said the older he gets, the less hair he has—that maybe he should eat more poi. He likes it. He said modern medicine has lots to learn from old Hawaiian ways."

Maile put her feet against the front seat, then let them slide to the floor. Dr. Tom sounded like a wonderful doctor.

Brooke pulled the neck of her T-shirt down. "See this?" she said, pointing to a small raised place under her skin, just below her collarbone. Her fingers skimmed the skin covering the bump. "With this, they don't have to poke my arms anymore. They use the port when they need blood. Or to give me chemo. The catheter goes in a vein all the way to my heart." She traced the route with her finger.

"Doesn't it hurt?" Maile asked, shivering. She felt like Charlie looked, and his face had turned green, as if he might be sick. He burped.

"They numb the skin. There's a little disc under here"—she touched the bump again—"where they stick the needles. They hang up an IV bag with the chemo inside and hook me up—drip the stuff in. It isn't so bad." Brooke straightened her T-shirt. She smiled. "They'll take the catheter out when I don't need it anymore."

Charlie held his hand over his stomach. Maile leaned away, just in case. It sounded terrible. She frowned. And something Brooke said wasn't right. *If Brooke didn't have any more cancer, why didn't they take out the catheter?* She didn't need any more chemo. Did she? Maile looked around. Hadn't anybody else heard what Brooke said? Nobody seemed worried. Brooke's uncle parked the car in front of Molly's Shave Ice stand as if everything were okay. "My treat," he said.

Charlie rubbed his stomach. "My opu feels better." He seemed glad to jump out of the car and stand on solid ground again.

"Rainbow ice, please." Charlie leaned against the counter as the machine shaved ice into fluff. "Make it big," he said, smiling.

61

"Mine too," Brooke said, getting in line behind Charlie. "Same as Charlie's."

"Passion fruit," Maile said when it was her turn.

Charlie sucked rainbow flavors from a straw stuck in the ice. Red and green dripped over the paper cone and down his fingers. Maile climbed back into the car. "Tutu Lady said to ask all of you to a luau next Saturday for Keoki." She crunched shave ice as she talked.

"I'd love to come," Brooke said. "Can we, Uncle Bill?"

Brooke's uncle nodded as he started the engine. "That would be nice. Please tell her yes, Maile."

"I bet Keoki will hunt wild pig for the luau," Charlie said.

"Oh." Brooke's smile disappeared. "But Keoki's so nice."

"Of course he's nice," Maile said. "He's my brother. He's the best."

"Then how come he hunts pigs?" Brooke asked.

Charlie took his glasses off and polished them with his sticky T-shirt. He held them up and squinted against the light, looking through the thick lenses. "You wouldn't feel bad if you saw a wild boar, Brooke. The males have tusks. They so ugly."

Brooke frowned. "They can't help how they look." She wadded the paper from her shave ice, red juice dripping from between her fingers. "How come people hunt pigs anyhow? Aren't they supposed to protect wild animals?"

"They kill them for food. Besides, wild pigs destroy

the old forests." Brooke made it sound like hunting was something bad. It made Maile feel all mixed up inside. She stared ahead as they wound along the beach road. Hawaiians had always hunted. Brooke just didn't understand.

For a second, Maile glanced at Brooke. She could see the bump from the catheter port just under Brooke's T-shirt. She looked away. Brooke must be lonely with just her uncle Bill, now that her mother was gone. Not that Maile would miss Brooke's mother, but Brooke would. Without any brothers and sisters. Or even a pet! At least Maile had Poi Dog. And Keoki—when he came home. And of course, Tutu Lady. What Brooke needed was a pet to keep her company. But even more, she needed something to help her fight cancer. So it wouldn't ever come back.

## 12

# The Beach by Aunty's House

**B**y the next morning, Maile had a plan to help Brooke. But she was so sleepy, she almost missed Keoki—before he left for the pig hunt. And he was part of the plan. The noise outside her window woke her up. The yard was full of hunters and dogs. Hunting dogs, yipping and growling. Maile opened her eyes. Poi Dog stood next to her pillow, growling. He nosed the window screen and almost pushed it off. Then she heard Keoki laughing outside.

She jumped off her bed and pulled a big T-shirt over her nightgown. "Stay," she told Poi Dog as she scooted out the front door.

"Wait, Keoki! Don't go yet," Maile yelled.

Keoki paused, holding a big box. "We wake you up? You look like one sleepyhead."

"I have to talk to you." Maile tugged on his shirt, trying to pull him away from the driveway, away from the hunters.

"Wait up, I'm coming," Keoki yelled to his friends. He tucked his shirt into his jeans as he followed Maile to the mango tree. "So what's going on?"

"Keoki, remember Brooke?"

"Of course I remember her," Keoki said. "Hurry up. Everyone's waiting."

"She could still be sick, you know," Maile blurted out. "And mostly she's alone at Hale Nani. Her mother only visits."

Keoki looked impatient. "Can't we can talk about this later?"

"We could help." Maile took a deep breath. "Please, if you find a baby pig, bring it back for her. For a pet."

From the driveway, the engine of a pickup truck coughed and started. An old jeep rumbled slowly down the cane road.

"The things you ask me to do, Maile," Keoki said, smiling. "I'll try." He turned and ran after the truck. In minutes the driveway was empty.

The sun climbed up over the mountains and painted the sky pink. It was hot already—a perfect day for the beach. Maile would be swimming with Brooke and Charlie in the ocean by Aunty's house while Keoki tramped around in the forest. It was lucky they were going, because that was the second part of the plan. There was something special about the pali, the cliffs, by Aunty's house. Someone lived up there. Someone who just might be able to help Brooke. Maile hurried back to the house.

"You want some papaya for breakfast?" Tutu Lady asked.

"Yes," Maile said, opening the screen door. She walked inside.

"I see Keoki got off okay," Tutu Lady said. "Those dogs make plenty noise." She reached for a jar. "Maile, take Aunty Abigail this guava jelly when you visit."

"Okay," Maile said, tapping her fingers on the table.

Tutu Lady cut the papaya open and spooned out the slippery black seeds. She put a slice of lime on the plate and handed Maile a papaya half.

Scooping slivers of golden-orange fruit on her spoon, Maile squeezed lime juice on top. It made her mouth water just to smell. She took a bite.

"You ever hear of an old man up on the pali by Aunty's house? Kids say he's a kahuna. A healer." Of course, none of the kids at school had ever gone up to see. They were scared. What if this guy was the kind of kahuna who practiced black magic and prayed people to death? Maybe that was why no one went up to see him!

"What man?" Tutu Lady rubbed her forehead, the place between her eyebrows where little wrinkles formed when she worried. And then the worry lines disappeared. "I know who they mean." She smiled. "He is a wise man. If you visit him, you must be very polite. In the old Hawaiian way."

"Like how?" Maile asked, frowning. Tutu Lady wouldn't let her visit the scary kind of kahuna. Would she?

"Well, don't stand in a rude way—no hands on hips, no folded arms," Tutu Lady said. "Don't pester. Wait for him to speak with you."

How could she remember all that? Maile sighed. Maybe it wasn't such a good idea, trying to find this kahuna man to heal Brooke.

The horn from Ratman's jeep blasted. Maile slipped into her bathing suit and pulled on her big T-shirt. Then she dashed outside to the jeep. She and Poi Dog jumped in the back next to Brooke. Maile set the jar of guava jelly on the seat.

"Hi, Ratman," Maile said, tapping him on the shoulder.

Ratman smiled at her. He turned the jeep on the ocean road, heading to Aunty's house. It was a short drive. Maile spotted Charlie waiting for them. "Thanks," she yelled as soon as Ratman stopped the jeep. She held the jelly jar high as she ran. Brooke and Poi Dog followed, leaping through the sand. The cliffs soared into the sky, making a jagged shadow on the beach.

## 13

## The Pali

*C*harlie wiggled the strap of his underwater goggles and looked longingly at the ocean. "I want to swim."

It was hot. Little rivers of perspiration ran down under Maile's arms. She wouldn't mind jumping in the ocean. She could go up the pali later, after getting cooled off. Squinting into the glare, she could see Aunty sitting in the shade of the coconut palms.

"If you want to swim, don't wait for me," Brooke said, her face pink in the heat. "I don't think I'll go. I have to wear clothes over my bathing suit. My medicine makes me sun sensitive. I'll look weird."

Maile and Charlie looked at each other.

"We always wear our clothes over our bathing suits. Everybody does," Maile said.

"Really?" Brooke asked, frowning.

"Almost always," Maile said.

Charlie pulled his shirt back on. "Right. I just didn't know we'd go swimming so soon."

Brooke pulled a bathing cap on over her head. She rubbed on sun block. Then they dashed across the hot sand. Poi Dog raced between them as they splashed into the ocean.

Wet coolness crept all around Maile, sneaking along her bathing suit, into the folds of her T-shirt. Treading water, she trailed her hands, letting the water flow between her fingers. It lapped around her face. She lay back, her hair streaming around her. Her T-shirt filled with air like a big bubble.

While Poi Dog nosed along the shore, in and out of the water, Maile, Brooke, and Charlie swam. Above them, the cliffs jutted into the sky.

"I saw a tiny fish," Brooke said, standing on the sandy bottom. "It swam between my fingers."

"Put your face in the water," Charlie said, "and you'll see more. Here, try my goggles. I can't see that great without my glasses anyway."

Brooke slipped the goggles on and put her face in the water. "Oh, wow!" she said, gasping when she came up for air. "My doctor has a little blue fish in his office aquarium—just like the ones here." She put her face in the water again.

Brooke and Charlie floated over the reef, facedown, blowing bubbles. It was time to go up the pali. It was a scary thing to do alone. Maile held her breath just thinking about it. But if the man on the pali was a real kahuna he might know some secret way to stop ~~Brooke's cancer from ever coming back.~~ She had to try!

Maile stood up, her hair sleek and wet against her neck, and walked out of the water, across the hot sand, straight to Aunty. Gathering the bottom of her T-shirt together, Maile wrung the water out. "Aunty, I'm going for a little walk up the trail there. That okay?" She was going to try to do all the stuff Tutu Lady told her about how to be Hawaiian, too.

Aunty leaned back, shielding her face when Poi Dog shook his coat. He sprayed her with salt water. "Take this wet dog with you."

Maile rubbed the sand off her feet and slipped on her thongs. She whistled. Poi Dog followed. Together they'd find this man she'd heard about. They started up the winding path.

As the trail grew steeper, Maile climbed more slowly. She could see the trail as it curved up and disappeared. The two dots in the ocean below, floating over the reef, were Charlie and Brooke. Maile wiped her face with her wet T-shirt. Where her bathing suit had dried, she felt itchy from the salt and sand.

Whew, it was hot. Poi Dog's tongue hung out as he scrambled up ahead of her. Up here, the trail turned into spindly weeds and pebbles. Maile wished she had a drink of water, wished she could sit in the green shadows on the other side of the rocks. But she climbed on, following the path by the edge of the cliff. She slipped, and her knees turned to jelly. Then she crouched, close to the ground; it would be easy to fall. Her heart raced as she inched along.

Finally she took off her thongs, holding them as she scrambled over tree roots and rocks. She could get a better grip going barefoot. Her feet just weren't used to shoes. She didn't remember ever going up so high before. Papa probably knew this place. He used to hike all over the pali. If only he were here now. Going up alone was a crazy thing to do. Suddenly part of the path narrowed and disappeared—the dirt had been washed away. Maile and Poi Dog peered over the edge. There was a ravine below. Maile shoved her hair away from her face and studied both sides of the trail.

She leaped.

With a dull thud, Maile landed on the other side. Solid. She made it. Poi Dog, too. Smiling, she started walking again. But the farther she went, the more she started to worry. What if the kahuna man only spoke Hawaiian? She wouldn't understand him, and he sure wouldn't understand her! It was fine for Tutu Lady to tell her "to be Hawaiian"—in the old Hawaiian way— but Maile didn't really know how.

When she looked down, she couldn't see the place where Brooke and Charlie were floating in the ocean. Everything below stretched out in various shades of blue—the sky and the ocean became one. A pebble, loosened by her foot, bounced off the ledge, clattering as it tumbled down.

Everything was quiet again.

Maile edged into the shadows by a grove of small

scrub trees. How far was she supposed to climb anyway? Hadn't she'd gone far enough? The thought of being up so high made her dizzy. Poi Dog had vanished into the bushes off the trail. Now Maile would have to find him. She wiped her forehead. If only it weren't so hot. She pictured herself with Brooke and Charlie, swimming in the ocean. She swatted a fly that buzzed her arm.

"Poi Dog," she called out. "Time to go." Rascal dog. As she went deeper in the underbrush, the trees seemed bigger. She shoved away some ropy vines and peered into the shadows. Poi Dog barked. She whistled.

He didn't come. What if he was caught somewhere? Maile pushed through the bushes. "Poi Dog, where are you?" She balanced on tree roots, slipping her arms around a tree trunk, trying to find him. She couldn't blame him for not bounding out when she could barely get through the tangled undergrowth. Sliding into a tiny clearing, she didn't notice anything odd at first.

Then she saw Poi Dog. He was pointing, the way hunting dogs do when they flush game. Maile took a step backward, slowly. The hair on Poi Dog's ruff bristled like the hairs on her arms.

"Who's there?" she yelled.

14

# The Shadow Man

"Who's there?" Maile called again, her heart racing. In the long strands of sunlight, all she could see was a dark shadow.

The shadow moved toward her. "Oh!" Maile said, stepping back, almost tripping. She could see a dark man with white hair. A shadow man, tall and skinny.

Poi Dog circled around him, sniffing. Between sniffs, he made little warning growls, but he kept his distance, never getting too close. Poi Dog was smart about things like that. Maile took another step backward. The shadow man came closer. Suddenly he stood next to her, his black eyes flashing.

"Mr. Pulani! I remember you." He used to talk story with Papa. She hadn't seen him in a long, long time.

But was Mr. Pulani a kahuna? "What are you doing up here?" Maile asked.

"What do you mean?" Mr. Pulani fanned his face. He sat down and leaned against a tree. "What are *you* doing here?"

"I'm looking for the kahuna," Maile said.

"Here?" Mr. Pulani looked surprised.

Maile twisted her fingers together. "Yes."

"Humph," Mr. Pulani said. "What do you want with him?"

Maile's legs felt like rubber. They simply gave way, and she flopped down next to Poi Dog. "I need to find one for my friend." She pictured Brooke on the beach with her bald head and the catheter bump hidden under her T-shirt.

"I need the kind who heals people. I don't want my friend's cancer to come back." The words stuck in Maile's throat. "And the regular doctors and the cancer doctors, well . . . they only give her checkups."

There was a long silence. Maile had wanted so much for him to be the kahuna.

"So you came all the way up here," he said.

"Yes," Maile said, her shoulders hunched. Poi Dog had stopped circling and growling, and sat down on top of Maile's foot.

"Maile Leilani Pihana Kahona McKenzie." Mr. Pulani said each vowel separately, softly, so Maile's name sounded musical, like the poetry Miss Hee read in school. But when Maile heard her haole name, McKenzie, her ears grew warm.

"Your papa sewed me together once." Mr. Pulani pointed to a scar on his leg. "He must miss this island—especially his children."

Maile turned away. The hurt welled up inside her like a big wave ready to hit the beach. She couldn't talk about Papa now.

"There are many ways to heal," Mr. Pulani continued, as if they were talking about other things, not Maile's father. "Of course, the hardest things to cure are feelings. Hawaiians have always known that." His voice had a strange soothing sound like ripples of water lapping the shore.

Mr. Pulani looked around the clearing and then back at Maile. "The one you seek lives in the valley where the taro grows."

"My valley?" Maile asked. It must be some other valley she didn't know about. Mr. Pulani talked the old Hawaiian way, like Tutu Lady sometimes did. What he said had to be figured out like a riddle.

"*To begin healing, one must forgive,*" Mr. Pulani said.

Maile blinked. That's just what her book *Old Hawaii* said about mending families, about using ho'oponopono. Maybe Mr. Pulani had read the same book! He must not understand—she needed help for Brooke. Not herself.

"Maile McKenzie, I hear you swim like your papa. You have many of the same gifts," Mr. Pulani said.

Maile remembered how she and Papa used to dive with the green sea turtles. Somehow the memory calmed her. She didn't often let herself remember the good things. But why did Mr. Pulani keep talking about Papa?

"Aloha heals many things," Mr. Pulani said.

"Thanks for helping," Maile said, remembering to be Hawaiian, to be polite. But what could Mr. Pulani know? He wasn't a kahuna.

Poi Dog barked out by the edge of the cliff. Maile turned toward the sound. When did Poi Dog sneak away? She looked around again, but Mr. Pulani had melted into the shadows. He'd disappeared.

Maile looked through the trees, around the clearing. She hadn't noticed how neat everything was—as if someone raked the dirt smooth—and the lava rock in one place looked almost polished. She edged out of the clearing.

Suddenly Maile stood in the bright sun, up the ledge from Poi Dog. She leaned into the prickle bushes, away from the cliff edge. Then she slid down, making little dust clouds as she moved from one clump of bushes to the next. And even though it was sticky hot in the sun, Maile felt a chill run down her back. Something was strange. How come a faraway place on a lava rock cliff should look so special? So cared for?

15

# Real Kine Aloha

It was late afternoon when they headed home in Rat-man's jeep. Making sure Charlie and Brooke were busy talking in back, Maile leaned toward Ratman. She tried to talk quietly. "Mr. Pulani told me about a healer in the valley where the taro grows. Do you think he meant my valley? Do you know if a kahuna lives there?"

"Your valley is special, Maile. I don't know about a kahuna. But the valley is a very Hawaiian place with real aloha—not like the paid-for aloha in the big hotels. The aloha in your valley comes from the heart," Rat-man said. "Love like that can be very healing."

Brooke popped up between the two front seats. "My uncle says that too."

"Tutu Lady has that kind of aloha," Charlie said.

Maile hadn't meant for them to hear! Some things were supposed to be private.

"Maile has aloha too," Brooke said.

Brooke thought that? Maile smiled.

Ratman's jeep turned down the cane road to Tutu Lady's house. Keoki stood in the middle of the drive.

"Keoki!" Maile yelled. She jumped from the jeep and ran to him. "I'm so glad you're back. How did the hunt go?" She lowered her voice to a whisper. "Did you get the little pig?"

Keoki smiled. "Sure thing. Only we have to hunt again for one big pig. For the luau."

"Oh, thank you!" Maile danced across the grass. Wait till Brooke saw!

"Brooke, your uncle said you can stay for supper," Tutu Lady said, "and spend the night. If that's okay with you."

Maile held her breath. Maybe Brooke wouldn't want to stay!

"I'd like that," Brooke said.

Maile grinned.

"We'll have lots of company," Tutu Lady said, "Ratman, Charlie, and Brooke. We can talk story. But first, I need help setting the table."

"Tutu Lady, what if I look at the little pig first?" Maile whispered.

"Maybe you set the table first," Tutu Lady said.

"It sure gets dark fast," Brooke said, looking out over the fields of cane. She helped Maile set the plates out on the table outside as the sun slipped behind the ocean.

"I'll light a kerosene lantern," Keoki said. "Brooke, Maile asked me to bring something for you from the forest."

"For me?" Brooke asked. "What is it?"

There was a snuffling sound from the pen by the shed.

"Come on!" Maile ran, leading the way, past the mango tree, past the poinsettia bushes, to the shed. Charlie and Poi Dog followed close behind. In a small pen, just as Keoki had promised, was the pig. It was already too dark to see clearly.

"Brooke," Maile yelled, dancing in the shadows. Why didn't she come?

"There's something hopping around on the grass, Maile."

Brooke must still be out on the lawn.

"Those are just bufos. Big toads. They come out every night."

"Yikes!" Brooke said, her voice rising.

"They eat the centipedes," Maile said.

"Centipedes, too? That's just great," Brooke said, as if she didn't think it was great at all. Outlined by the light from the house, she stood like a statue, with toads hopping around her.

Maile wound her way between the toads to Brooke and grabbed her hand. She tried to lead Brooke across the lawn. Brooke didn't move. She was stuck in the grass like an anchor caught on the reef.

"Just tell me what Keoki brought," Brooke said. "I don't need to see it."

"You need to look," Maile said.

"It's dark."

"Hold on, Brooke." A path of light moved across the lawn. Keoki swung the lantern. Only, in the light, the toads looked bigger. Their shadows stretched across the grass and into the night.

They'd never get Brooke to move. And Charlie wasn't any help—he made spooky faces in the lantern light.

From the pen came a soft, whimpering sound.

"What's that noise?" Brooke asked. And to Maile's surprise, Brooke followed Keoki. Step by step. When Keoki stopped, Brooke stopped.

Little grunting noises came from the pen. Then a mournful cry.

"Oh!" Brooke ran then, ignoring the toads and the dark shadows. Poi Dog was already by the pen. He sniffed between the slats.

Keoki held the lantern high. The flame sputtered, then glowed bright.

Brooke leaned against the fence. "It's a little pig!" She turned, her eyes sparkling. "She's for me? I've never, ever had a pet before. Oh, Maile . . ."

Maile smiled. "You won't be lonely anymore, Brooke."

Brooke climbed up on the rail next to Charlie and Maile. The three of them peered down into the pen. A little black pig stared back.

## 16

# The Cure for Being Lonely

They ate supper near the mango tree. Maile squeezed in between Charlie and Brooke on one of the long wooden benches. Brooke sneaked off two times to share food with her little pig.

At the end of the table, Ratman passed the bowl filled with sticky rice to Keoki. "How'd the hunt go?"

"We went up Henderson tract. Plenty pilikia, plenty trouble, from wild pigs. They root up nearly everything." Keoki looked across the table at Brooke. "That little peeg, she plenty smart," he said, lapsing into pidgin. When he talked to Brooke, he used less pidgin, like turning down the volume on the radio. Maile did, too. Only sometimes they forgot.

"Pigs are smarter than dogs," Charlie said.

"Some dogs," Maile added. She reached under the table and petted Poi Dog. He could be very sensitive.

"Did you find my pig there, at that place called Henderson's?" Brooke asked.

Keoki nodded. "In the fern forest." He leaned forward, his elbows on the table. "The ferns shoot up, oh, some twenty feet, like trees. The fronds grow so close, the rain falls as mist, and the sun looks green. The ground is spongy and soft. It makes you bounce when you walk."

"So that's where the wild pigs live," Brooke said softly. "It sounds beautiful."

Keoki nodded. "Prehistoric. Sacred. Only pigs, they like eat fern stem. It kills the fern trees. So we hunt. But pigs live plenty places, Brooke."

Tutu Lady tapped her spoon on her water glass. "We're happy Brooke has her little pig."

"What are you going to call her?" Ratman asked.

"Plumeria Rose." Brooke giggled. "This peeg is a numbah one peeg."

Maile and Charlie giggled. Brooke sounded like a local girl. Like she belonged.

"It was an honor to catch this peeg for you, Brooke," Keoki said, bowing in his chair.

"Tell us about the pali today, Maile," Tutu Lady said.

Everyone turned toward Maile, laughing and joking.

"The pali behind Aunty's house?" Keoki asked.

Maile nodded. "I learned something new." In her

mind, she trudged up the pali again. She told them about the climb and the view and meeting Mr. Pulani. "I was looking for a kahuna," Maile said. "A healer." There wasn't any reason not to say. Not now.

"Mr. Pulani said there's a healer in the valley where the taro grows. Do you think he means our valley?"

Keoki and Tutu Lady looked at each other as if they knew something they weren't telling. Maybe they knew who the healer was! Of course, some things were secret. But Maile could keep secrets. It wasn't fair not telling her.

Now, though, Brooke was here, and it was time for bed. Ratman drove Charlie home. At the tiny bathroom sink, Brooke and Maile washed up. Brooke chattered about Plumeria Rose.

When they turned out the light in Maile's room, Brooke grew silent. Tiny dots of light from the living room glowed through the termite holes in the wooden wall.

"Look," Maile whispered as she knelt by the wall, Poi Dog at her side.

Brooke crouched beside them. In the living room, Keoki and Tutu Lady sat on the couch watching television.

"If the termites ever stop holding hands, our house would fall down," Maile whispered, grinning in the dark.

Brooke nodded. "We've got termite holes at Hale Nani, but they aren't in my bedroom. The ones you have are great. You can see everything."

"It's good ventilation, too. Good for a hot night. With so many holes, the breeze comes right through," Maile said.

Brooke peered through the tiny holes. "We'll be able to hear Plumeria Rose, if she cries in the night."

"You can sleep in my bed," Maile said. "Tutu Lady put fresh sheets on." Maile unrolled the sleeping bag on the floor for herself.

Suddenly the room went dark. The tiny pinpoints of light from the living room disappeared. They could hear Tutu Lady and Keoki going off to bed. There was a dull thud on the ground outside.

"What was that?" Brooke whispered.

"Just a mango falling off the tree," Maile said as she smoothed out the bumps in the sleeping bag and lay down. Poi Dog snuggled next to her.

The room was silent.

"Are you sure?" Brooke asked.

"Yes."

"Maybe we should check," Brooke said. "Or turn on a light. Are you thirsty? I am."

Maile sat up. "I'll get you something to drink."

"I'll go with you," Brooke whispered.

"No. It's okay." Maile scurried out the door as fast as she could. What if Brooke followed? As soon as they turned on the kitchen light, the cockroaches would run everywhere. Maile knew they would. Tutu Lady swept the crumbs up every night. She scrubbed the counters. Maile took the garbage out. Sometimes it worked, and they didn't see any bugs for a long time. But sometimes it didn't work. Cockroaches liked to make plenty noise. They rattled inside cellophane wrappers. Or paper bags. She could imagine Brooke if that happened!

When Maile got back with a glass of juice for Brooke, the bedroom light was on.

"Guess what I found, Maile! A pile of old letters. They fell on the floor when I moved the mattress up to make it straight." She held the letters up. "I think maybe one is opened. And Maile, they're all addressed to you!"

## 17

## Letters

*O*h no! Maile's heart pounded so loudly. The letters!

Sitting in the middle of the bed, Brooke scanned the postmarks. "Some of these letters are two years old."

"They're from my papa." Strange how far away her voice sounded, as she were in a tunnel. Maile leaned against the bed.

Brooke spread the twelve unopened envelopes across the sheet like as if she were dealing cards. "Don't you want to know what he wrote?"

Maile scooped up the envelopes. "I read one."

"Did you write back?"

Maile shook her head. "No."

"But what if he stops writing because he never hears from you?"

Papa might, too. He'd stopped calling when Maile wouldn't talk on the phone on her birthday. Maile felt cold, remembering.

Brooke leaned on her elbows and rested her chin on her hand. "What if something terrible happens? You'd never know."

Brooke was making such a big deal about everything, assuming the worst. "He writes Tutu Lady."

"Maybe he sent you money, Maile. You might be rich. My father sends money to my mom all the time. Court order."

Maile sat down on the bed. Poi Dog stretched. He leaned against her legs. She didn't care about money. But what if something had happened to Papa? Suddenly she didn't want to wait anymore to read the letters. She took an envelope and tore it open. She ripped them all open, one by one. The letters lay in a little cluster by the pillow. There *was* money—a five-dollar bill.

"Don't feel bad, Maile. Some fathers are stingy," Brooke said when she saw it.

Maile raised her eyebrows. Papa wasn't that way. He sent a little money to Tutu Lady whenever he could.

"I'll stay awake if you want to read them, Maile. It's better to have someone with you when you hear bad stuff."

"You don't have to do that," Maile said.

Brooke fluffed the pillow and lay down. "I won't tell anybody anything, Maile. Some stuff is private."

"It's really late." Maile reached over and turned the light off. She lay down on the sleeping bag next to Poi Dog, the letters clutched in her hand. She stared into the darkness.

"You promise not to tell?" Maile asked.

"Of course," Brooke said.

"No matter what they say?"

"I promise."

"Are you sure?" Maile asked. Could she trust Brooke that much?

"I'm sure," Brooke said.

Maile got up and turned the light on. Then she and Poi Dog climbed up next to Brooke. The three of them huddled together. Brooke spread a bathrobe out like a blanket to cover their feet. Holding the first letter up to the light, Maile began to read aloud. " 'Dear Maile, I miss you and Keoki.' " He missed them! " 'How is Poi Dog? And Tutu Lady?' " For a minute, she could almost see Papa standing before them. " 'Study hard. Love from your papa.' " Maile held the letter close. "Love," Papa had written.

Brooke yawned. Maile felt foolish. To anyone else, Papa's letter would seem like an everyday kind of letter. What was she afraid of all this time? For two whole years! She read three more letters. The letters all sounded sort of the same—still, they were special. There was even a letter from Papa's wife, Danielle. " 'Dear Maile, I hope I get to meet you,' " it began. Fat chance, Maile thought.

Poi Dog started to snore. Brooke lay her head on

the pillow. Her eyes kept closing. In fact, she looked as if she were sleeping. Maile didn't care. She kept reading letter after letter out loud. " 'Dear Maile, I moved again.' " His newest address was Oregon. Papa sure moved around a lot. Too much, Maile thought. " 'Please understand,' " she read, " 'why I had to leave you. . . .' "

"What?" Brooke asked, sitting up straight, her eyes wide open. "That's the awful part, isn't it?"

Maile nodded. Suddenly it was hard to talk. " 'I needed more training so I could get a job that pays.' " Maile laid the letter down. He had a good job now. But he'd already given Maile and Keoki away. Thank goodness for Tutu Lady! So good she was.

"Don't feel bad. My father divorced us. I used to think it was because I got sick."

"You couldn't help that!" Maile said.

"I know that now. But I didn't before. The counselor at the hospital talked to me. And it isn't your fault that your papa left, Maile."

"Are you sure?" Maile asked, her head low. She'd always thought Papa must be angry at her, that she was too much trouble. Brooke was the first person she'd dared to tell.

Brooke pulled more bathrobe over her legs. "It wasn't you, Maile. I bet if you ask Keoki, he'll tell you the same thing."

"You really think so?" Maile blinked back tears. Then she took a deep breath. It was nice to know her family wasn't the only mixed-up family around. Brooke's family was, too.

Brooke nodded. "Yes, I do."

Maile picked up the last letter. " 'Dear Maile,' " she read, " 'you still mad?' " So Papa knew. " 'We'll be visiting the island soon. We want to see you.' " They might be here. Papa and Danielle. Papa knew Maile was angry, yet he still wanted to see her. Did she have to see them both? Maile didn't care about seeing Danielle. Maile turned the letter over.

"Oh, no," Brooke said, sitting up straight. "When did he write?"

Maile read the letterhead. "August second."

"Hmmm." Brooke started counting on her fingers. "That was three weeks ago. Oh, Maile. What if he already tried to reach you?"

A lump grew in the back of Maile's throat.

"You should call him," Brooke said.

"I can't," Maile said, trying to swallow. "It costs too much."

"I've got a long distance card," Brooke said. "I get a special discount. This call's on me. I owe you for all the poi."

Poi Dog and Maile tumbled off the bed. "You'd do that for me?"

"Of course! I know what it's like to be away. I have to call all the time." Brooke dragged the bathrobe after her as they ran into the kitchen to the phone. "Just don't talk a long time."

Brooke dialed her card number. Maile hung back. Everything was happening too fast.

"Come on. You'll need his number when I finish," Brooke said.

Maile rummaged around in the kitchen drawer for Tutu Lady's list of telephone numbers. But when she dialed, her fingers fumbled. She hung up. It would be easier to talk if she was alone, but she couldn't very well ask Brooke to leave. Not when she'd been so nice. Brooke dialed her card number again. Taking a deep breath, Maile dialed again too. This time, the phone at the other end rang. And then she heard Papa's voice.

She clutched the receiver tightly. "Hello, Papa." But the voice on the other end kept talking. "Leave a message at the beep. We'll return your call as soon as possible."

"Papa? This is Maile." Her voice cracked. But the beep kept going on and on. Sighing, she laid the receiver down. "The tape needs to be fixed." She felt hollow inside. Empty.

"Never mind," Brooke said. "We can try again another time. Or he might call before we do. Did you ever think of that?"

That night Maile rolled about inside the sleeping bag. The floor felt hard like aa, the stony kind of lava rock. Twice she banged her elbow against the wall.

Early the next morning, a coconut crashed to the ground outside the window.

"Maile?" Brooke called from across the room. "Hear that sound?"

"Coconut," Maile said, yawning. Wasn't it too early to wake up?

"Oh. I was thinking about that man you met on the pali. Mr. Pulani. I don't think he was talking about a kahuna. He said *healer*, didn't he? There're lots of different kinds of healers." Brooke sat up on the bed. "The healer could be anyone in the valley. Your valley, Maile. You never know!"

Maile smiled. Maybe Brooke was right. Wouldn't that be the funniest thing? A girl from the mainland figuring out something like that? She slipped out of her sleeping bag. Strange how good she felt. How happy. It was fun having someone over to spend the night. She pulled on her shorts under her oversized T-shirt. Brooke slipped into her striped shorts and matching top. She hopped across the room, barefoot. Poi Dog thumped his tail on the floor.

"Do you think Plumeria Rose is okay? She's probably lonely. Let's go check," Brooke said. The three of them thundered through the house and out on the porch. Poi Dog barked as they leaped off the steps.

"Come, walk with me," Tutu Lady called to them from across the lawn.

They ran to her. "We're going to see Plumeria Rose," Brooke said.

Tutu Lady nodded. "I'll go with you." With her arms around Brooke and Maile, they walked together to the pigpen. "I had a wild pig once. A little one, like Plumeria Rose," Tutu Lady said. "I called him Blackie. He was the cutest pig. So tame. He followed me everywhere. I'd say, Blackie, lie down. And he would. I'd say, Blackie, come, follow me. And he did."

"Oh, that's wonderful. Will Plumeria Rose be able to do that too?" Brooke ran ahead. "Do you think I can teach her?"

Tutu Lady smiled. "Yes. I think you've got one smart pig."

"We have to take her up to Hale Nani," Brooke said. As if Plumeria Rose understood, she wiggled her snout between the slats of the pen. Brooke leaned down and petted her.

Maile looked inside the pen. Plumeria Rose had beautiful long eyelashes. She was so cute. It would be fun to have a little pig. But she couldn't imagine Poi Dog and a pig together. Poi Dog was already jealous of Plumeria Rose.

Maile jumped up. She didn't have time to fool around. Papa was going to call. Taking Plumeria Rose to Hale Nani would take a while. Maybe a long time. If they were gone too long, she might miss him. "Tutu Lady, if Papa calls, I want to talk with him this time. If I'm at Hale Nani, please tell him to try again."

"I'll be weeding in the garden, Maile. I can run inside. But if we miss the call, he'll call back."

He might not though, Maile thought.

Brooke opened the gate just a crack. Maile leaped forward, but Plumeria Rose slipped through. Maile had an armful of nothing. She landed with a thud on the ground. Plumeria Rose kept running through the tall grass and disappeared.

## 18

## Plumeria Rose

**M**aile lay on the ground for a minute. She sat up slowly. That little pig moved fast!

"What'll we do now?" Brooke asked.

"Let's try some mango." Maile picked a rosy-yellow fruit off the tree. She set it on the ground by Brooke. Maile edged away toward the side of the house.

Brooke made a soft crooning sound. In a minute or two, the little pig peeked out from the tall grass. She looked all around. Finally, she trotted over to the mango. Maile edged into the shadows by the side of the house. It was taking forever. At least here she could hear the phone, if it happened to ring—if Papa called.

From the overhang above Maile's head, a gecko clicked and scolded. He flicked his tail. Maile looked back at Brooke and Plumeria Rose. Maybe if she sneaked back, she could help Brooke get Plumeria Rose into the wooden box Keoki had set out in the driveway earlier that morning. If Plumeria Rose didn't run away again. Maile crept along the side of the house. Plumeria Rose turned, just the tiniest bit. She was so quick. But this time, Brooke caught her and held her tight.

Together Brooke and Maile lifted the little pig into the box. Her snout quivered from between the wooden slats. She cried. It was a pitiful sound. Brooke reached down into the box to pet her.

When Keoki swung the box up into his old rusted jeep, Plumeria Rose squealed again and again. Brooke sat in the backseat by the box and talked to her little pig all the way to the plantation house. Maile sat in the front and smoothed Poi Dog's coat. He was every bit as cute as Plumeria Rose.

When they got to Hale Nani, Maile and Poi Dog jumped out. Plumeria Rose watched them through the slats of her box.

"So where do you want to keep your pig?" Keoki asked.

"Inside," Brooke said.

Maile raised her eyebrows. Inside Hale Nani!

"Tutu Lady told me she used to keep Blackie in her house," Brooke said.

Maile stuck her chin out. Tutu Lady was always telling Maile to put Poi Dog outside.

The screen door opened and Mrs. Kohara, the housekeeper, ran down the front entrance steps to the jeep. "Did you get enough sleep, Brooke? I told your uncle you shouldn't stay overnight. That you needed your rest." She looked Brooke up and down. "What happened to your leg?"

"Just a scratch," Brooke said. "Mrs. Kohara, do you know Maile and Keoki?"

Mrs. Kohara nodded. But she didn't look at them. Instead, she stared at the little snout wiggling through the wooden slats of the box Keoki carried. She put her hands to her head like she had a bad headache.

Brooke said, "This is my pig, Plumeria Rose, Mrs. Kohara. Keoki found her in the fern forest." She led the procession up the walk to the big house.

Mrs. Kohara ran around in front of them and blocked the way. "Not in the manager's house. Not inside!"

"I'll fix something outside," Keoki said, setting the box down.

Brooke stopped. "But Maile got her so I won't be lonely."

"What would your mother say if she found a pig living in the house?" Mrs. Kohara asked.

Maile looked at Brooke. They grinned. Somehow, they'd have to be sure to get Plumeria Rose inside Hale Nani before Brooke's mother came back. Maile imagined Brooke's mother meeting Plumeria Rose in the hallway some night. Maile giggled.

For the rest of the week, Maile helped Keoki fix up around the valley house. It was only right. After all, he got Plumeria Rose for Brooke as a favor for Maile. So she didn't complain when Keoki wanted his jeep washed, and together they mended screens and fixed loose boards on the porch steps. It was a perfect time to ask Keoki lots of things. Personal kind of things.

Maile held a board steady as Keoki hammered "Did you ever try ho'oponopono?" she asked finally. She wanted so much to learn more about it.

Keoki laughed. "Sure. I was one rascal. Tutu Lady and me, we did a lot of ho'oponopono. Especially after Mama died. You were too little then to know what was going on. It was an everyday sort of thing. And then, sometimes, too, after Papa left." He raised the hammer. "But it only works if people forgive each other." The hammer came down hard on the nail.

"Did you ever try ho'oponopono with Papa?" Maile asked.

Keoki hammered in another nail. "Tutu Lady did."

Maile's mouth fell open. "Why didn't you ever tell me?"

Keoki gave Maile a look. "You didn't let anybody talk about Papa. Remember?"

Maile remembered.

Keoki set the hammer down. "When the sugar plantations started to shut down, Papa lost his job. He couldn't find work. He disappeared for days. Weeks. He'd fish, hunt, hike the pali.

"Tutu Lady took care of us," Keoki said, looking at Maile. "That's when she and Papa agreed to ho'oponopono. To set things right."

"Did they use a mediator?" Maile asked, trying to imagine Papa and Tutu Lady talking things out together. They would have needed a referee. But who did Papa know? Then she remembered what Keoki had just said, about Papa hiking the pali. She knew Shadow Man was Papa's friend.

Keoki nodded.

"I bet it was Mr. Pulani."

"How'd you guess?"

Maile grinned. "I just did. You know, there's something strange up on the pali. There's this one place. It looks so cared for. In the middle of nowhere! You ever notice that?"

"Yeah, I have." Keoki put the hammer down. He looked at Maile. "Sometime when you swim by Aunty's house, look at those cliffs from the water."

"I've seen shadows up there." Maile's mind raced. "Oh, Keoki, you think they're caves?"

"I think so. Mr. Pulani might be a kahu, a guardian, for some ancient grave, some sacred place."

"Tutu Lady said he's a very wise man," Maile said. Suddenly it occurred to her that it didn't matter that Mr. Pulani wasn't a kahuna. And that what he'd said about healing was probably true.

# 19

## Green Mangoes

**O**n Friday, everyone squeezed into the tiny kitchen of the valley house to make laulau for Keoki's luau. Everyone except Keoki. He was off hunting again, for the luau pig. But Rosemary was there. Charlie and Brooke. Maile and Tutu Lady.

"We'll teach you how to make laulau, Brooke," Rosemary said.

Charlie stood by the table. "Production line."

Brooke smiled. She sat at the table near Charlie and watched.

"I spoon meat and fish on top of the taro leaves." Maile spread the giant heart-shaped leaves out on the countertop.

Charlie rattled a bowl of red salt. "I sprinkle Hawaiian salt on top."

Rosemary folded ti leaves around the packet Maile and Charlie put together. "It's like wrapping a present." She shredded a long fiber from a ti leaf and made a bow.

"Some are almost ready to try," Tutu Lady said, looking at the big pots filled with laulau, cooking on the stove. Clouds of steam filled the air.

In all the noise and confusion, Maile almost didn't hear the phone ring. It sounded so muffled. She looked at the counter, where the phone usually sat, but somebody had moved it. "So where's the phone?"

No one seemed to hear her. They were all too busy. Bent over a laulau packet, Brooke was busy wrapping. Rosemary had uncovered the big sheet cake she'd baked at home. In script, she was writing *Aloha Keoki* in blue frosting across the top. Charlie and Tutu Lady worked at the stove, half hidden by the clouds of steam.

"Does anybody know where the phone is?" Maile asked again, louder.

Everyone moved in slow motion, turning to stare. "What?" Rosemary asked.

Tutu Lady pointed to the chair. "Look over there— under the phone book."

Maile's heart pounded. Maybe the phone had already stopped ringing. She shoved the phone book aside and lifted the receiver. "Hello?" She wound the telephone cord around and around her fingers. "Papa?" she asked.

Maile looked around. Rosemary had started making rosebuds on the cake. Charlie stared out the window. Brooke kept wrapping laulau. She was almost hidden by the pile of laulau packets. But Maile was sure they were all listening. Even Tutu Lady.

"No one's there." Maile hung up. She turned away and faced the wall.

"Your papa will call," Tutu Lady said, giving Maile a small hug.

"Maile, you and Brooke should dance hula at the luau," Charlie said.

"I'm not any good," Maile said.

"I can ask Aunty if she'll dance with you. When it's time to dance, just follow what she does. You'll do fine," Tutu Lady said.

Maile's face grew warm. She wished she danced often enough to be good. Like her mama had been.

"I'd like to learn," Brooke said.

Tutu Lady nodded and then looked at Maile. "For Keoki, okay? And Aunty. You'd make them both happy."

"For me, too. Please," Brooke said.

"Okay," Maile said slowly.

Rosemary gathered her things together. "See you tomorrow. Don't let Keoki see the cake."

They started to straighten up. Maile could see Rosemary out in the yard, packing her things in the trunk of her car. Maile washed the pots and pans used in making laulau. She leaned against the sink. Charlie and

101

Tutu Lady dried. Brooke shoved chairs back around the table.

After a while, Charlie hung the towel up that he'd been using. "Hey, we're done here. I'm going outside." He shoved the screen door open. "Coming?"

"In a minute," Maile said.

"Why don't you go with Charlie? The tree on the hill still has some green mangoes. You know how he loves them," Tutu Lady asked.

But Maile hung back. She'd been so sure Papa would call.

Charlie peered in through the screen. "When are you two coming out?" He held up a long bamboo pole with a net at one end. "I found a mango picker."

Charlie and those green mangoes! Maile smiled. She pushed thoughts about Papa away. She and Brooke ran outside. The three of them raced across the grass and down the dirt road. It felt good to run. Poi Dog loped along beside them.

Charlie balanced the bamboo pole over his shoulder, the scoop net dangling back and forth as he ran. He dashed off the road and up the hill to a giant tree. While he waited in the shade, he called out, "Slowpokes!"

"Charlie, don't forget what happened the last time you ate too many green mangoes," Maile said when she reached the tree.

"What happened?" Brooke asked, breathing hard after the run.

"Stomachache!" Maile held her middle. It was no wonder with all that Charlie ate. He'd already packed the bottom of his T-shirt with mangoes, and they'd only just started picking.

Brooke worked on the fruit on the other side of the tree. For a minute, it was just Maile and Charlie. Like old times.

"Your Papa doesn't know what he's missing, Maile," Charlie said, "or he'd be here. He'd call every day."

Maile's chin trembled. She turned away.

"Hey, you've got plenty friends," Charlie said, chomping down on a crisp green mango. "Let's go." He tried to keep his shirt wrapped around all the mangoes he'd stuffed inside it.

They started back. Maile started to run, but carrying mangoes slowed her down. This time it was Brooke who carried the mango picker, balanced across her shoulders. Poi Dog raced ahead. They followed, walking through the cane fields, the tassels blowing in the wind. Maile could almost smell the laulau cooking. Her mouth watered. She squinted into the afternoon sun, glancing at Brooke. She looked again. And then she stopped so fast, the mangoes she carried bounced out of her arms.

## 20

## The Opu Huli Lady

"**B**rooke, your hair is growing!" Maile danced along the cane road in between the mangoes she'd spilled. There was touch of golden color on the top of Brooke's head, like down on a baby bird.

"I can't see any hair." Charlie squinted, the late afternoon sun glinting off his glasses. With one arm, he clutched the green mangoes wrapped in the front of his shirt, and with the other arm, he shielded his eyes.

Brooke smiled. "I was waiting for you to notice."

"It's beautiful, Brooke," Maile said.

"Now I can see something," Charlie said.

"It's a start." Brooke nodded, feeling the top of her head.

Maile picked up all the mangoes she'd dropped.

Then they walked down the dirt road. She kept glancing over at Brooke's new hair and smiling. Charlie started to eat another mango. He stopped. "Hurry, Charlie," Maile called out. She'd never seen him walk so slowly. She couldn't go fast herself, carrying mangoes. But for someone who usually went faster than everybody, he moved like a snail.

Maile and Brooke scooted on ahead. They were out of breath when they got to the house. They sat at the table with Tutu Lady, waiting. When Charlie finally arrived, he dumped his shirtload of mangoes into a big basket.

Tutu Lady gave them each one laulau. "To taste," she said.

In a flash, Brooke unwrapped hers, leaving a big pile of ti leaves on the side of her plate. "Yikes, it's hot!" She blew on her fingertips. Then she took a bite of laulau. "I like it."

So surprised she sounded! Maile unwrapped her own laulau. She could easily eat two. "The fish is good in here. The pig, too."

"Oh." Brooke looked up. "I didn't think about the kind of meat we used."

"I only just thought of it myself," Maile said. She felt bad for Brooke. Everybody always loved laulau.

"It's okay," Brooke said. But Maile could tell it wasn't. Brooke ate the fish and the taro leaves but not another bite of pork.

Charlie stood up and walked around the table. "I don't feel like eating now." He sat down on the living room chair. He had a green tinge just as he'd had when he'd seen Brooke's catheter bump. And he'd always loved laulau. He'd probably eaten too many green mangoes again.

"Don't get sick," Maile said. As if that would stop him.

"You want to lie down?" Tutu Lady asked. "Maybe have some tea, settle your opu?"

Charlie curled up on the living room couch, his back to them. "I'll be okay."

Maile cleared the table and dumped the ti leaves into the garbage. Tutu Lady filled the sink with water and started to wash dishes. Brooke grabbed a towel.

"You all right, Charlie?" Tutu Lady asked.

"Not yet," Charlie said.

"Maile, why don't you call Ratman? Ask him if he's coming by," Tutu Lady said.

Maile lifted the receiver to her ear. "Our phone's out again. Someone must've hit the pole. I'll try later."

What if Papa tried to call? With the phone out?

"It's cold in here," Charlie said, sitting up on the couch. "I'm going outside on the porch." Maile, Brooke, and Tutu Lady looked at one another. Cold? It was hot. Through the window screen, they heard Charlie groan.

Tutu Lady dried her hands and went out on the porch. Brooke and Maile stood in the doorway, watching through the screen door. Tutu Lady felt Charlie's forehead. "Maybe we need to take you to Opu Huli Lady. Make you feel better."

"What does Opu Huli Lady do?" Brooke asked.

"She straightens stomachs, if they get turned around," Maile said.

Brooke frowned. "Turned around?"

"She does a little lomilomi, a little massage," Maile said. Her own stomach wobbled at the thought.

"Shouldn't we get him to a real doctor?" Brooke asked.

"If he needs one, Opu Huli Lady will know," Maile said, looking outside as the sun set. Brooke didn't understand. But even the clinic doctor respected Opu Huli Lady. It wasn't such a crazy thing. They'd been through this with Charlie two times before. Charlie and green mangoes. You'd think he'd learn.

"Try the phone again, Maile," Tutu Lady said from the porch. "Let Charlie's folks know, too."

"All right." Maile walked to the phone and lifted the receiver again. Nothing. No sound. Of all the times for Keoki to be off hunting. "Keoki should be here any minute with a pig for the luau." She peered at Keoki's parked jeep in the growing darkness outside. She wished he'd hurry. If he didn't get home soon, she'd have to drive.

"The phone still doesn't work." Maile opened the screen door and went out to the porch. Brooke sat on the steps near Tutu Lady. In front of Charlie, the moon sat on top of the betel nut tree, balancing like a big balloon. Charlie looked awful in the moonlight.

"I should have learned to drive long ago." Tutu Lady patted Charlie's face with a towel.

"I can drive Keoki's jeep," Maile offered. She was

a good driver. Even Keoki said so. "It isn't far to Opu Huli Lady's house. Maybe five minutes. Not even that."

"Can you reach the pedals?" Brooke asked.

"Sure," Maile said. She just had to stretch a lot.

"Let's get Charlie in the jeep," Tutu Lady said.

"We'll do okay," Maile said as they helped Charlie.

"And I can help," Brooke added.

"I'll try to reach Charlie's folks. Opu Huli Lady doesn't have a phone. I'll send Keoki as soon as he gets here," Tutu Lady said. "He'll find you."

Charlie curled up in the back. Maile scooted the driver's seat up and put the keys in the ignition. Brooke climbed into the passenger side as Maile turned the keys. Only, nothing happened.

"You've got to step on the gas," Brooke said.

Maile shoved her foot down on the gas pedal. The engine roared. Down on the clutch, get in gear, up on the clutch. She remembered! The jeep lurched forward. Then, the engine shuddered and died.

Maile tried the key again and switched on the headlights. She shifted and pressed down on the gas pedal. Harder and harder. This time the engine hummed. They rolled down the driveway. Maile peered into the night. Pop. Pop. Bufos exploded under the tires.

"Gross," Brooke said.

In the headlights, they could see rows of toads, armies of toads.

"Plug your ears!" Maile shoved her foot down hard on the gas pedal. They left the drive. Pop. Pop.

The jeep bumped through the cane fields, racing, skimming the rows of cane. As they rode through the valley, the air felt cooler. Cane stalks towered over the road. Light from the headlights bobbed up and down as they moved into the darkness. It was scary driving at night. Maile gripped the steering wheel tightly. Whenever they hit a bump, Charlie groaned.

"We're almost there," Maile said. She wished Charlie wouldn't groan like that. It made her nervous.

Brooke peered through the windshield. "I can see a roof."

The jeep lurched along the road. In front of them was a little house surrounded by ti plants—ti plants to keep the bad spirits away. Dogs barked.

"How many dogs does she have anyway?" Brooke asked.

"Plenty," Maile said. "They let her know when someone comes."

As they slowed, the jeep seemed to jump. It stopped. Maile and Brooke looked at each other. The door of the little house burst open. Light from inside spread over the ground. And suddenly, blocking the light, there stood Opu Huli Lady. For someone so big, she moved quickly, gracefully. Her muumuu swirled and billowed as she rushed to greet them.

"Charlie ate green mangoes again," Maile said.

Opu Huli Lady wiped Charlie's forehead. Then, she held her hand over one side of his stomach. She drew it back sharply as if she'd held it over something hot. A spasm ran across his stomach. Like a muscle twitch.

"Maile, take Charlie to the hospital *now*," Opu Huli Lady said.

It wasn't green mangoes after all. Charlie was really sick!

"You come too," Maile said.

"I won't fit," Opu Huli Lady said.

It was true. She was no small lady. She'd get stuck for sure. Brooke crawled in back to sit next to Charlie. Maile turned the keys in the ignition. This time there was nothing to it.

The engine sputtered. Maile pushed her foot down on the gas pedal and eased up on the clutch. The jeep sprang forward. And once again they seemed to fly over the dirt road.

They turned onto the paved road, the highway into town, empty in the moonlight. Maile's mind raced. Where was the healer Mr. Pulani talked about anyway? When they needed one? They passed the grocery store, the bank, and the laundry. Nothing was open. They climbed the long hill to the hospital, in the same low gear, all the way. Charlie groaned again.

Maile aimed for the big EMERGENCY sign by the entry doors. She pressed down hard on the horn.

Together Maile and Brooke pulled up the emergency brake as a nurse ran out to meet them.

"Tell my mom and pop, okay?" Charlie's teeth chattered. The nurse put him on a gurney.

"Hey, you're going to be okay," Maile said. He *had* to be!

And then the nurse wheeled Charlie inside.

## 21

## The Luau

The next day, at the hospital, Charlie's mom and pop made a big deal about Maile and Brooke.

"Heroes," Charlie's dad said.

The doctor praised them, too. "Charlie's lucky to have such good friends."

Maile looked at the pole next to Charlie's bed with the skinny plastic tubing looped together like limp spaghetti. The place smelled antiseptic, like the lab where Ratman worked. "How you feel now, Charlie? Without your appendix, I mean." She leaned against the bed. She wanted to touch his hand, but there was all that tubing coiled around his palm.

Charlie yawned. "My opu feels like someone

punched me." Then he closed his eyes and fell asleep—
right in front of everybody.

Maile and Brooke tiptoed out of the room and
walked down the hall.

That night at the luau, everybody wanted to hear
about the wild ride through the cane fields, and how
Maile and Brooke saved Charlie. It would be easy to
get a swelled head, talking so much.

Tutu Lady kept them busy running and carrying
platters of food: sweet potato, shrimp, fresh pineapple,
mangoes, coconut pudding squares served on banana
leaf. More and more cars and trucks arrived and parked
around the little house. Everybody was there. Except
Charlie.

When Aunty Abigail arrived, she hugged Maile and
then Brooke. "So nice of Tutu Lady to invite me to
dance with you." She gave them each a tiara made of
tiny blossoms.

Then they watched Keoki as he strummed his uku-
lele. People sang and talked and ate. Smoke rose from
the underground oven—the imu.

In the food line, Maile took a scoop of sticky rice,
some kalua pig, and a paper bowl filled with poi.
Brooke took a second helping of the fish marinated in
soy sauce with grated onion on top. "I love this stuff."

Maile grinned. "That's raw fish, Brooke."

"So?" Brooke took another bite.

"Hey, I like it, too," Maile said.

Under the mango tree, Keoki's friends sang Hawaiian songs. One after another. Their strong voices rose,

higher and higher. They sang of the sea, of cowboys riding into the mountains, love songs, lonely songs. They made up songs for Maile and Brooke. "Two little seestahs," they sang.

The torchlights flickered. "You're so lucky," Brooke whispered. "You have such a big family." She leaned back against the bench where they were sitting.

"Me? All I have is Tutu Lady, Poi Dog, and Keoki—when he's here." Maile frowned. "That isn't a big family." Poi Dog helped. She leaned down and petted him.

"You forgot Aunty Abigail—she's family. And you've got plenty of friends—Charlie, Ratman, and me! It seems like a big family." Brooke grinned.

"Aunty's not related. She doesn't have any nieces. No kids even." Maile watched her aunty and Tutu Lady laugh together. Maile turned to Brooke, then looked back at Aunty and Tutu Lady again. She started to smile. "They're like sisters."

"One seestah?" Brooke asked, giggling.

"Yeah, what you think? Maybe you and me, we could be sisters, too." Maile waited. What if Brooke didn't want to be sisters?

But Brooke made a shaka sign—just like a local girl! She stuck out her thumb and little finger from her fist and waved. "Right on," she said.

Maile made a shaka sign back. A sister! She wanted to leap in the air.

They giggled together as Aunty Abigail walked toward them. "Time to hula. Don't be nervous—just listen to the music," she said. "For Keoki we dance."

113

Maile and Brooke copied Aunty. If Aunty's hands "talked," their hands "talked" too. Maile's hands circled her head and shoulders, becoming the moon. She pulled an imaginary fishing line, then she put her hands out and wiggled her thumbs imitating a fish swimming in the ocean.

Aunty turned to the right. Brooke and Maile took two steps to the left. Same time. Nobody seemed to mind when they crashed. They laughed instead. Really good Brooke did, first time hula. Maile looked out at everybody—so many smiling faces.

Aunty bowed. They stopped dancing. People clapped. It was over—too fast, Maile thought.

"Maile, phone call," Tutu Lady said.

Maile seemed to float across the yard and into the house, her heart beating fast. "Papa?" she asked when she picked up the receiver.

"Maile." It *was* Papa.

"Oh, Papa." Maile didn't know where to begin. "When do you come?" she asked finally.

"In two weeks. How's that sound?"

"Really good." A lump in her throat made it hard to talk.

"We'll stay one week, maybe a little bit more. Is that okay?" Papa asked.

"Oh, yes." Maile sat down suddenly.

"You want anything from the mainland, Maile? Something we could bring you?"

"No. But I need to ask something." Maile took a deep breath. "I want to set things right between us.

Like you and Tutu Lady did long ago." Papa didn't answer. Maile clutched the receiver. She felt as if she'd slipped off the pali and was falling, around and around in the air.

"That's fine, Maile." Papa's voice sounded sort of rough. Like he might cry.

"Really?" The spinning stopped.

"Papa, you still like green mangoes?"

"Of course," Papa said. "I like them best dipped in a sauce Tutu Lady used to make—a little shoyu, vinegar, some sugar. She still make it that way?"

"With a dash of black pepper, too," Maile said. "Our tree out back has the best mangoes anywhere." Suddenly she could hardly wait for his visit. "Aloha, Papa," she whispered when they finished talking. For a minute she stood, holding the telephone receiver before hanging up. Papa's picture. It would look nice on top of her bureau. *Maybe* even that picture of him and Danielle together. Someday she'd tell him how she and Brooke saved Charlie. How she drove Keoki's jeep. She'd tell him lots of things.

Maile ran out of the house and across the grass. She tapped Ratman on the shoulder. "Can I ask a favor? Would you help me work things out with Papa when he comes?"

"I'd be proud, Maile."

And whereas before she would've said "Thanks, Ratman," now she said, "Thanks, Uncle." She smiled at the sound of it.

He did, too.

115

"You want to dance some more, Brooke?" Maile asked.

Brooke shook her head. "I want to watch this time. You dance, Maile."

"I dedicate this dance to my family," Maile said, looking out at all her friends. "And to Charlie and Papa, who can't be here. For Mr. Pulani." Maile couldn't forget Shadow Man. She felt better already, even though, so far, she'd forgiven Papa only the tiniest bit. Mr. Pulani had said you had to forgive first—before you can heal.

Alone in the moonlight, she started to dance. She felt pretty, like people said her mama used to look.

There was a hushed silence.

She imagined Mama dancing. The two of them together. She could almost hear the ancient chants. An ancient drum.

"Huli," Maile called, turning. Like she was sure Mama used to do.

Smiling, Maile drew her arms close to her heart and then lifted her arms outward. "*Aloha*," she said. "*Aloha nui loa*." The best medicine of all—the Hawaiian words for love.